w a s

was

MICHAEL JOYCE

FC2
TUSCALOOSA

The University of Alabama Press
Tuscaloosa, Alabama 35487-0380

Published by FC2, an imprint of the University of Alabama Press, with support provided by Florida State University and the Publications Unit of the
Department of English at Illinois State University

Address all editorial inquiries to: Fiction Collective Two, Florida State
University, c/o English Department, Tallahassee, FL 32306-1580

⊛
The paper on which this book is printed meets the minimum requirements
of American National Standard for Information Sciences—Permanence of
Paper for Printed Library Materials, ANSI Z39.48–1984

Library of Congress Cataloging-in-Publication Data
Joyce, Michael.
   Was : annales nomadique/a novel of internet / by Michael Joyce. — 1st ed.
     p. cm.
   ISBN-13: 978-1-57366-137-9 (pbk. : alk. paper)
   ISBN-10: 1-57366-137-6 (pbk. : alk. paper)
   I. Title.
   PS3560.O885W37 2007
   813'.6—dc22
                                    2006029962

Cover Design: Lou Robinson
Book Design: Joe Amadon and Tara Reeser
Typeface: Baskerville
Produced and printed in the United States of America

was: *annales nomadique*
a novel of internet

This, after all, is Jeremiah's book,
"Electronic Boy" having become documentarian.

I dreamt that I was held to
Creating a libretto
For music that flowed evermore

Anna Akhmatova, "Poem without a Hero"

.

was thought not were the yellow the irrepressible ever who said who said ends Ashtoreth one Wednesday, one Wednesday in June the damp the dampness in everything (light, profusionist, no I mean heat)

forty times now, bowing, clogs along foggy bottom news from the front, wooden boxes neatly in rows

the last the lost wandering *allées* (lips pressed to the neonate's skull, powder scent) willows all now gone from their ripeness

and what of the stipple, the limp, the lost what-was, despite the damp odor of canvas, the salt-cracked lips, inordinate corridors? who can say who can say

distant machines growl through *die Nähe (durch)*

she goes out

she goes out again

bereft, put-upon the dogs circle, their bloodied knees glistening damply

along thought now, begins with if, not begs as he misread,
and if, so considered, say sawdust sausages and diesel fumes
or the faded parasols and flutes of Prosecco, silver bucket of
sardines *sur le quai Branly*, too tardy to set off, redolent of inte-
riority, thinking, thinking a seizure, a pleasure, a string purse,
the death of a tiny thing, a beetle without a common name,
bloodless, foxing the endpapers of the calf-bound 12mo of
Terence's *Comoediae* she brought back from Caracas, if then?
how to live, I mean.

I mean I mean

again she goes out, *la charrada (charros y musica)*, amusing herself—etymologically so, things

neighborhoof, once misspoke, *l'amuse-bouche*, cherry lipped

global creolization = URL

olé olé, under skirt's goat beard, almond scent, headcheese

benign complication, dramatis personae: *due*, viz., the dan-
tesque: "*volentier parlerei a quei due*"

hears a good story

set forth a skiff doomed to barratry, fouled in her scuppers, seacocks seized with velvet rust, tulipwood planks damply aromatic, porpoises abeam

land locked look at her thighs, the seas the seasons by the lee, I, no, nothing, pink drinks on ice, tumblers sweating feathers, elliptical palm leaf shadow, the Tamil princess's teeth shredding sugar cane (*Gramineae Saccharum officinarum*), those days glorious, glint of the chalice held aloft in pink manicured fingers, sentimental gangster (hums)

> *Milonguita,*
> *los hombres te han hecho mal*
> *y hoy darias toda tu alma*
> *por vestirte de percal.*

saxophone portico and lurid petticoats, echoes languidly intrude, relentlessly not making sense, what else is music, Davide amigo?

dead plastic telephone, curiously cocoa stained basalt

head inland

katabatic gusts rising up into the lowering overcast, winds through the pass, winds pass, winds past, whistling

hangs in, spake the man at the bar, eruption unregistered, barrista's overlapping swirls yawning, tamps a mahogany *kafé*, MTV on the telly

Jó napot kívánok. Egyetemista vagyok. Everything means something to someone: waterfall pinball music, the Gigue Fugue
of Bach on a mobile phone

suckling creature tucked under her blouse, vaguely marsupi-
al, mounts the steps of the trekker's Toyota jitney, backpack
squarely situated

last night's knifing bloodless, gibbous moon, potato and ramp
frittata bubbling in lard, yet no one moves

bakelite (corrects him) no matter, the fat bloom whitish upon
a block of ghosted Oaxacan chocolate, say, *La Soledad* or
Guelaguetza, now a miraculous photograph *de la La Virgen de
Juquila*, three euro, mister

my seester

the dog's abrading tongue, the nun like a dirigible, this way
and that

pyramids of Calabicita, black radish, *Thymus praecox*, slum-
bering peaches, melon gash crawling with dark winged rai-
sins

let's get out of here, let's

yes

refugee consciousness, a radio lozenge, certain unforeseen
cul de sacs, multicolored phone cards and the right festive
hat, motor vehicles bureau, sultry white presidio

I want to waltz once

more.

slow descent of the mothership over the dry lake bed, a miraculous pouring forth, distant murmur, an empty stadium, all we have lived for lost, or who can tell (so irritable, she says), the hovering shade offers a welcoming respite, for once almost making sense, sweet shoots stir themselves, labial: cumulus

under the shadow their shadows lost, one two three, one, two three, one two

the same train arrives seven times running *am Bahnhof*, each time the same cast and crew disembarking, east time he thought, as if a film loop, *La Ciotat* et alia, nervous conductor tapping the crystal of his wristwatch, endless recurrence no excuse, Togolese redcap's soprano sax aria, *Agapornis pullarius*, 1964 definitive, listed at 200 francs, the coolness of the glass arcade after the compartment

prandial shuffle of cards, *sept de cuillères*, watches her sway across the plaza, shadow oblique, unveering

hesitation about trusting casement, compass, snapline, pencil (rayograph salamander their logo; slogan unknown), physics of a pawn shop diffraction grating, small town diadem, blue chalk measure of an afternoon

the precision of ennui, this moment, this (sways unveering), x7

SMS = telegram

postcard of a *parcheggio* in Rifredi (*Line Firenze-Pistoia-Bologna*)
4.5 km from the Uffizi, asphalt inscribed with graphically
crisp hatching, Egyptian temple facing the *laghetto*, Hellenis-
tic temple beyond the lemon trees and the stables, off-duty
gypsy woman napping on the lawn, Hogarth's Curve, loss of
innocence perpendicular to the descent of narrative *dans le
rêve lucide*, lacks patience with this and who can blame

will you love me?

when?

and again the day begins without summoning, sun wandering purposelessly, is of course its purpose, such cleverness at
breakfast, laughter like ice cubes on the hotel terrace, tarry
cigarettes, corporate countess with a harlot's lips, pert breasts
neatly packaged as twin gabardine parcels, belted waist,
Blackberry tracking satellites from a clutch purse, toast crust
detritus, neatly ringed crimson cork tip filter deftly swept
away, smoothes skirt abaft, aright, moves off

no nightingales in the new world, the Polish poet said, this
is a problem (rueful smile, dark-haired wife midway in the
auditorium), nor do your blackbirds sing

harbour seals venture far up the river

it is no matter

though you would think it otherwise it is impossible to see oneself in the mirrored surface of a CD, she said, incorrectly it turned out

it has been good

then what, the fog riven into drifting forelocks, dusty stones *come pane casareccio* in the morning sun. (then and what) two and a half hours before noon and, acedia, a name for every thing, waft of cloacal salt scent *il Palazzo Contarini del Bovolo*, faraway Veneto, distant Ophir, *dopo* an hour before coffee again makes sense, until then (here is the origin of art), driftwood twigs twirl languidly in opalescent oil skim, beard of yellow pollen clinging to them

(then what | when that), i.e., global reversibility of cellular automata, viz., unidentified middle-age man of uncertain nationality wearing yoked gingham cowboy shirt plus Teju lizard boots with hand-tooled and painted uppers, duty-free at Schiphol shopping for salt licorice

16 min

the longing for event weighing on his shoulders like a field piece, *crus ansata, fissura coronalis*, good shepherd, a lace of bloody sweat on his forehead, it is a long story, a lonely motorcycle along a nearby stone *passaggio* soon lost, the transit of venus accomplished nightly via nickel-chrome alloy cylinder tumbling slowly through arid darkness, graphite composite and epoxy skin pinging @ thirty cycles per second, Dasabimbaras approaching the threshold of the universe (it

is all very exciting but his companion, imagining the smell of
straw, longs to breathe the air outside the dark theater)

baptized Eve, awkward embarrassed rictus one finds charming (rehearses the possible replies: atom, atman, admin, ad
man, *al-atwah*, haha), smiles

(Advert: Reinforcement works from 8mm Ø to 42 mm Ø any
size or shape, subcontract ok.)

greeting grasps his hand longer than one might, softly softly

Christian, spoken as if giving her a small coin

do you like to coffee? is not how it is said (as if in a sea or a
game)

has a story begun then?

Once a time was and a met strange near the far in land,
windshield wiper flaying, failing, clay smears splay across
semi-clear orbital segments, grouse tail, cloud abyss, bus engine knocking, dozing in the scent of cloves and perspiration,
soft breast against the *Brachioradialis*, ear pillowed against the
Serratus Anterior, a/k/a boxer's muscle, the world will always
welcome, time, goes

on a spherical plane a vast molecular crowd, garnet muscovite
olivine suspension, a loose particulate upon an excited surface, sand spew, awaiting the sun's returning, sharply dancing
crystal soldiers, commoners, defrocked geomancer spitting
tobacco (viz., *Scytodes thoracica*) to whom it's all a game

he detests children, spat likewise

unruffled awaits, she tranquil (at the bottom of the nubbed espresso cup a beach of chocolate sand, feeds it to herself on narrow spoon, *corpus corporum, amen*

amen

unblinking

recapitulates, inside this mote (so pronounced) a scream and, of course, the head; but then, thus far that is, love isn't in question, for naught all the goings and coming soon what next (it's annoying, meaning boring the way one announces it), a heaviness at her center as if suddenly putting on weight, leaden swallowing, cramps perhaps or dawn, a limp worm, snoring, sickening wafts of fermenting honey or sperm, a sliver moon, sets, while she

sleeps

no referents, *sans Giovanni* or the muse of Calais (a blind stab), we are left unturned, no twins on opposite shores, hithering, apophatic yawn, yet you are well educated, one day quotidian bibliographers will explore the disappearance of the cross-country bus ticket as a cultural form (spondee giving way to dactylic), but what of the sinew? the sense of the

calligraphic nonsense on boxcars, ptyalizing boys, ratio of perfection, and in the tunnel nothing but the dull gaze, face to face ("believe," fr. 138) outside the coach the rail clack, *cara*

Doricha, in the window of the future someone will remember, believe, belief, shot forth to light and her face erased, a smear of pallid green replacing its features, iron colored lake's dark and ragged edge where the eye was

finally, disguised by dreams, they arrive, a hundred years old now, carrying their house rolled up upon their back, rotting sail, boots coming apart at the seams, sunken eyes, his limp useless smile, the dormitory in the hostel smelling of chlorine bleach, men on cots crying out for wives, a smokestack at some distance spells out its black litany against a yellow sky and through the walls someone, in the shower a woman, siren, sings, "the oak's deep heart and the fisherman's oar," Mandelstam's song of wood

that's the story of, *la gloire de*, rendezvous aborted, e.g., Sasikiran v. Harikrishna, Qb2+, one night paid but left (1) cot untouched (2) half-uncial note at front desk (= blue's traveler tune, avs.): *xtian no hope no rescue eve*, (3) plum lipstick kiss infra sig., wax faintly bergamot (disinterested clerk watching Canal+ reality teevee, deposed, gestures toward the only door apropos), all night through the darkened quarter spiraling toward the terminal, teenage hookers in glitter-dusted Diesel knockoffs and open-toed sandals sipping soft drinks through colored straws, sickly colored dawn striated sherbet parfait, skipped westbound train and waited for the east, retracing last night's, missed, last, -30-

she saw him off from a distance

FF: a city like London but not (cf. Lubjana, Lexington, Lahore, Lisbon), still a river, "picturesque" brick towers, pomo mews, Bauhaus quays, disneyfied Futurist ferris wheel, nightly fireworks, shops *avec panini*, flavored soaps, hand rolled/hand tied jasmine balls in green glass replica apothecary jars, *Kanom Krok* smoking over coals, Pig Snout on the tap

the inevitable turn toward narrative: c.v., blogspot MISPER report, vacuous profile cum dubious photo, nostalgic burnt ammonia smell, Marconi Wireless cablegram, urgent uppercase, carbon-stained finger whorl, clerkly diction: anent which else such *oder sonst noch so gibt, u.s.w.*

symmetries of pavement or work for hire, dispatches from a series of cybercafes, *neti-neti* returned-replied to, pinging the aether, bcc litany: St. Jude patron of lost causes, St. Anthony patron of the lost, St. Margaret of Antioch, *ora pro nobis*

full six months in a shared flat with an office girl named Devi, each other's refugees, not barring the occasional brush up against, frying cauliflower, green cardamom seed, assiduously lotioned, scrawny flanks, wept in sleep, awoke lucid to the touch, savory nubbed disks of sable soft upon her chest, rising, dark eyes as the story goes, fond of Blandy's Rainwater Madeira, apt to claw thereafter

seldom herself entertaining friends behind closed doors, mobilely upward once insisted earnestly

left one day and didn't come home, both of them

12 pp handwritten life story—austerely looping inked pea-
cock-blue cursive courtesy Little Flower Convent Girls High
School, Guruvayoor, Kerala—in his Invicta backpack

packet of lavender pastilles on the sideboard wrapped in
pink ribbon

for her part Eve disappeared staying where she was, a ser-
pentine stratagem, looping back on one self, cf. "genuine
Christine," bifid, i.e., licking once own ouns with (width?)
doubled tongue, sleeps lightly moaning; amoan, the worm
turns, viz., Voltairine De Cleyre (1900), the bird of omen

panhandle, shovel, whiskbroom, fraying denim over ankle
length khaki, hitech breathable hiking boots, constellation
Andromeda ikat indigo bandana

bitch, puta, kutu, Hure, *Durga Tripura Rahasya*

bedding down in matted grass beyond a cane fringed swale,
pale straw swirl where deer lay down, river smell and musk
and tiny violets, precise hopping of winged creatures branch
to branch, moonlight frottage and vacant dreams: scow sighs
and rising, moans against the hawser, ghosts pass along the
trail in single file, dimly phosphorescent, lowly crooning,
the breath of them like smoke, silent owls devour steaming
mice

in the black glass of the acrid pool Hecate's sunken eyes,
mask of oxblood clay where the lover has sealed them

I left you to love

awoke to dog's tongue and vagrant frond of hot sun across
her face, the hound nuzzled into complicity shushed, ranged
sniffing still back toward the master's orbiting call, a herd of
dull tin bells baahing at some distance, limbs aching, hiss of
melodious piss at the trunk of a beech tree, its accompanying
perfume, ankles itch, dried smears of grey mud at hip and
shoulder brush easily off, morning toilet (a girl's dream of
coloring the lips with berries)

she resolves to find a path to the city and become a private
secretary

or to find

something beyond the damp stiffness of sleep will not ease in
her hip, left, arthritic she supposes, aching rotational sense of
the socket itself, a wiry spike of pain with each footfall: *Dzién
dobry, prababka*, made a salve of comfrey cooked in butter and
rubbed it on the hip, tissue thin hands caressing the girl's
flank over and over again, *cicha woda, cicha woda, serduszka*, in
English: darling, darling, *chrzesniaczka*, dear godchild, what
has happened to us

years pass implacable as flowers, the architecture of Babcia's
bony shoulders familiar beneath the washcloth imbued with
pungent Czech soap, yet not nursing but nursed, in retreat
from, not love, but the constancy of emotion, learning (*via neg-
ativa*) non-ness and *patientia*, the imagined rustic cottage a flat
in a dreary brick and glass socialist tower, hallway smelling of

chrzan (sharp root) and *kapusta*, the inevitable cabbage—and yet

and yet Babcia kept a bony milkgoat (*koza*) in a shed toward the back of a friend's weedy lot, zealously wished the girl could find a *polski chlopak*, Polish boyfriend, and for hours on evenings after Angelus passed her time before the television whispering the names of things, filling the child's ear with the honey, *miod*, of the mother tongue

iPods, she had read in the newspaper, scientific proof, sapped the brainwaves of the young, siphoning memories to the stratosphere, downloading (speaking the word in English: down low) *Polski Rap—Zakazane Piosenki*

forbidden songs

spits: *Dzién Szaka-l'a-Bafangoo*, as if the name of Satan, crossing herself (saner than some, no crazier than most)

life in a suburb, *tesknota*, viz., *saudade*, "a sorrowful longing," a series of digital cellphone self-portraits, no one calling, email as pointless as Babcia's rosary beads, a shelf of canned soup above the stove

lingering once—the young priest making a surprise visit in his blue cassock and retro biretta—she list from the steaming bath as his soft tone and Babcia's singsong wove, the flesh along her thighs pink with scald, her breasts buoyant

that night resolved to dream this, without result

months later, once upon a time, finding a gauze packet under her pillowcase, a charm of rose hips, lavender buds, and bay leaves tied with a pink ribbon, in the morning made a tea of it, Babcia silent over dry toast

smiling once upon

perhaps imagined you would outlive her, as if in a fairy tale or a bus schedule, 22:13; 22:21; 22:30; 22:47, driver having a smoke in the night, the cloud above him blank panel of a comic book, glaciers afloat on themselves

or follow reindeer into Lapland

she answered the phone and he was not there, clutched a fist between her thighs, Babcia's clear glass rosary wrapped around her fingers, cold

borrowing a cardboard suitcase smelling of death and camphor, vicinity by definition where one has stayed too long

for his part skated, nearly four hours daily, northward also along interconnected rivers, wife slung on his back like a parcel, sharp heels checking against his waist, warm circle of her breath on the back of his neck freezing into a silver medallion, twin babies crosswise seal pups at her breasts

Hans Brinker along the Rideau Canal, it is all made up, still the weight of it, the push of lost love, real, limestone turrets rising into view message in a dream, empty dial tone

on a bus among pilgrims (Santiago-Mendoza) harrowing Los Caracoles switchbacks Cristo Redentor tunnel, *salve regina, vita dulcedo*, Germans snoring unperturbed, among *gli altri* one lost cause, blind drunk moaning, turns out to be an American mercenary, whispering with the border guards, machine guns swaying at their hips, laughing aloud as he boards the next bus back

thinks to join him but the guards are suspicious and will not hold the bus

Los Penitantes, San Martin de los Andes, Las Islas del Sol y de la Luna

Nordic skis sold in Mendoza to a befuddled Huarpe vendor in the Mercado, taking the next bus back, the same yawning teenage *protector de la frontera* as the day before, finger on the trigger, staring and then, *vaya vaya*, sullenly tossing the passport back across the formica

daytripper, *mula quizás*

four successive days arising before dawn in the hostel dormitory, thimble of *agüita* or peppery chocolate in the maze of streets near the *término*, diesel aroma of the idling autobuses, and every morning the American soldier already there, feigning drunken slumber before stumbling onto the Mendoza bus, twice looking back on the fifth day taken in for questioning

(*en español*) what's the story, *chacotero?* you some *copuchento*, eh *fleto?* some things you cannot know

(protesting) *soy un payado* (in English) busker, you know, mate

the strumming gesture in air

¿Verdad, huaso? where's your guitar (laughing), in Mendoza with your skis?

no drugs in his pockets or backpack, no payback in planting it, day wearing on

face slap hard enough the marks last an hour

vaya, asshole, stay away from the bus station, *¿Entiende?*

¡Y compre una guitarra!, shouts the pimply fucking *milico*

cabros, boys, laughing together, sun already high

days later on the plaza the same American soldier in a clean white shirt

1500 km National Road, No. 3, cab of a Word of God truck driven by a local *taquillero* playing Christian hiphop, i.e., Gosepl Gangstaz and KJ-52, jumping out along the Patagonia coast, at the bottom of the world seabirds, cellphone useless hello hallo echo

a constant roaring, lace lapsing over stones, rumors of dolphins

stock up on Montecol bars and bottled water, thereafter (*oficina municipal Puerto San Julián*) calquing: *Perdóneme por favor, yo desean caer en amor*, pardon me, I wishes to fall in love

to fall, *tu falle*

je ne sais past

bus sliding off the road margin on a high pass, tumbling end on end, *et in saecula saeculorum* (no longer operant)

amen (a boy's fantasy, we proceed more slowly to our death)

one sole story (sensei): "the hitchhiker or the wormhole in the universe" (The Shipman's Tale a variant)

a virgin whisper proffers comfort beneath her skirt but no room within her, soft descant (not descent) of angels sotto voce

the third glorious mystery our lady's retro-evolution, closed lotus bud of undeveloped vulva per deci-bead interval

sealing up her opening with damp mud, desiccate vespid queen (a/k/a nest mother) awaits the end of winter (December, tierra del fuego) a longing for

him, for her

cut to: the chase (Saint Castin and other stories, viz., "waiting woods, sensitive in every leafless twig in silence and dim
around a lodge"), a new world

what are the conversations besides bed? (beside her low bed a
waterglass, full, citronella candle, unlit, a yellowing notepad,
pencil mamilla, balm of Gilead, devout comix)

where are you from what was how long have you were you

(used to have a different name she forgot) chilblains, goblins

only wants someone who can promise a year or more of hap-
piness (to or from whom?)

yes, exactly

code of courtly love (C++), *chanson ordinateur de Guillaume de
Machaut*: Ballade: a a b (or, if a = ab, then ab ab c), Virelai: A
b b a A b b a A, Rondeau: A B a A a b A B (humming Sting's
song: *La belle dame sans regrets*)

void dummyfunction (void)
{
cout <<

"tu brises mon coeur, je pense, tu sais, erreurs, jamais";

repeat: *encore une fois*

mendicant couple wending way northward, immaculate conception, *via liebre* (the rabbit) and hitchhiking

kiss me (but then I only want to touch you)

kiss me but do not

kiss me

beginning to think she's a Maryknoll (merry laughter)

sans wimple, ex-communicate, vide Heloise's *vale unice*, cf. "farewell my all"

(one can be overeducated, this a simpler tale: e.g. Dogme 95: The Vow of Chastity #6, no superficial action)

more simply then: sinew thread shred of dark meat finger of bitter herb mild cheese smear palm leaf wrap *maíz* (tamale?) steamed and served from a sack at his waist like a ball park hot dog vendor

then a little farther on and equally unlikely: 99er with a Flake (stump like a wartime amputee) as in Beach Break Cafe, 158 Kings Road Arches, Brighton, Isla Malvinas

the now and then of comestibles, *brewis* of unknown shell-fish, coelacanth history (you had to be there)

Wenders, W., End of World

before until then after now

once while

a simple sister outlasting him

a decision, *theatre du soleil à la Cartoucherie (Paris)*, to keep her body to herself a full year at a time, thence regularly assess her progress

five years passing, lifespan of the white nun finch ("not typically a bird that should be handled...if breeding is undesired, females may be kept together without difficulty...doing best with covered nesting")

aspires to become a bleached smooth stone high on a beach

frescoes of swallows (dateline *La Nation 31.01.05: convento de Santissima Annunziata y la actual sede del Instituto Geográfico Militar*) convent where Leonardo lodged (now a military college)

body lighter than air, *Luftschiff*, lover (sisters of the holy spirit)

squat among the ladies of the village looking at them looking at her looking, pass small cloth sacks of coca leaf and *legía*, Pachamama radio waves, scrubbing the green stain later with a worn toothbrush, mirror's morning gilt face *ikon Axion estin*

bussing tables ecotourist cruise ship Ushuaia to Antarctica (1200 km 8 days, via Drake's Passage), jumps ship Paradise

Harbour, Deception Island, attempting (unsuccessfully) to disappear, apocryphal reappearance Medjugorje (Bosnia-Herzegovina) years after

Gabriel de Castilla-St. Kliment Ohridski (via the supply ship Hesperides)

blinking bespectacled graduate student, a boy with yellow hair, Pozy Botev, politely extending an ungloved hand, a nickname for *poezia* (poet)

Khristos, he explained confusingly (they resolved to exist in two languages, university English and supply ship *español*), was famous *poezia* (poet) *¿Entiende?* (embarrassed in two languages, each cheek red)

hearing "Christos bowtie," she laughs, the boy's cheeks beet dark

her wish, to stay, sweetheart or sister as you wish, latching on somehow, impossible

are you married, she asks

betrothed, Kira, a medical student in Sofia

summer's last ship, I promise, she says (crossing herself right to left, Kira Khristos, throne of Christ)

I can cook, I am a nurse, I sing.

seeing him hesitate, offers to sleep on the floor of the generator room

asks, sweetly, to see her passport, studying her eyes like a customs agent

will have to speak to the authorities (yes, yes, of course, but later, she whispers, so weary)

the world's bottom span a difficult transverse, yet stranger things have happened, hissing comets for instance, or how one day they found the icy corpse of a Russian floating on the bay

now a disembarking goddess in a borrowed parka, hitchhiking missionary, sailors' concertina, supply ship scullion, call her what you will, Venus and Sigma Octantis in conjunction

wakes that night aware of the boy on the floor rubbing himself in the dark (having insisted she take the cot, a geologist by nature) her heart aching for all faraway lovers

summoned commissary morning head of station evokes common sense authority: "now you are here, miss, and so what can we do?"

next boat she promises but when it came and went she moved instead into a supply closet, declining warmer arms, other offers of shelter, waiting out her vow, took on tasks without being asked, swept scoured bandaged simmered vats of makeshift soup, picked up a few Bulgarian phrases, *izvi-nete, molla, blagodaria, izmoren li si? az sam tvoiata maika zavinagi*

I promise I promise

walking along the barren rocks with the other woman there, Boulissa, aptly a hydrologist, laughing, sharing sweets, sweet kisses, fervent Sephardic prayers, Ladino folk tales, dreams of several futures

once when there was still magic in the world, in the cool of a movie house on an afternoon in a provincial equatorial town, the tale-teller Tonik held softly the damp hand of her orphaned daughter and dreamt Cinderella anew, turning her mind to the story in the midst of a technicolor adventure, allowing the ballet of snorting horses, flapping cavalry flags, and the saccharine soundtrack to drift out of mind, the telling coming to her with a truer eye than the tracking shot

Maria the swine butcher's daughter, likewise an orphan, runs chitterlings through her fingers, scrubbing blood and plucking specks of scum and yellow fat; putting them aside she is pounding fragrant *maíz* for tortillas when an old man appears and offers her a blue brocaded Zinacantán sash with magical powers to do her work for her while she attends the fiesta, a shining star on her forehead, dancing Ladino style with the prince (cf. the witch's broom of various bedtime stories)

silver sandal lost, how they spun, happily ever after, yet by some accounts "still working because she was used to it" equilibrium of stories, orphan to orphan, dance to dance, a daughter's hands, fatherless succession, *kuy*➜*j'albe*

(cf. Anna Moffo to Isao Tomita, via Rachmaninov's *Vokolij*)

entering into her 60's, the seventh sun in 10 Manik, in the Mayan Year of 10 Ik at the beginning of both the white man's millennium and the last 13-year cycle of the Mayan Long Count Calendar, Maria Gloriosa Sanchez Nibak has come by Trailways bus from Chiapas, Mexico to Poughkeepsie, New York at the urging of her son Jagu, a lawyer and community activist, after retiring from her work as a teacher at *El Centro Estatal de Lengua, Arte y Literatura Indígena (CELALI)* and following his divorce and heartbreak

Jagu did not meet the bus and there was no bus station so Maria Gloriosa walked through the abandoned downtown on her own, finding before too long a Oaxacan delicatessen where they called the restaurant (El Bracero) where Jagu was drinking Tecate and he came to get her, full of tears and apologies

perdóneme mami, teléfono célular

all this is fairly straightforward, reverse appliqué, village life, a mother's burden

the twins, *los gemelos*, Chaco and Elena *con su madre, si, buena, buena tambien, ambas, si*

buena buena todos in the city *norte*, the river Hudson low and dark under the bridge beyond the railroad tracks *mami cansada*

twin stars Chaco y Elena in each other's arms

woke shivering under the Huipile patchwork, Jagu snoring in
another room, and, dressed in her best double-breasted linen
suit and ivory pumps, went out looking for her grandchildren
and before too long a stranger, *una hermana de la luna*, gave her
a coat to wear in the cold spring morning, and not long after
that an H-man with two yellow teeth and a face of wrinkled
tobacco arroyos led her to them where they lived, *los nietos
gemelos*, leaving her with a sack of *pulpa vero* candies before he
disappeared into the sky

they were not home, of course, *dek-a dek-a* a neighbor woman
explained

I speak English, *Hablo ingles*

dek-ka, dek-ka, day care, mama working, *si* (ate the candies
and waited, *una tía* bringing her tea on the doorstep, read a
pamphlet of poems snatched from the shelf at Jagu's titled
"Men Love Chocolates But They Don't Say"

before long Jagu comes up in a taxi, riding in the backseat
like a priest

viene a casa, mami

abuela

the cabdriver grinning out, ebony face white teeth flashing
gold

bone joor Andre, she say, how you know (*comment vous savez mon
nom?*) say he

an old *bruja*, Jagu explains, and they all laugh (neighbor ladies out on their steps with the sun)

what you want then, okay, Jagu says and they drive away
again, a little later Andre returns with a sack of *sopas con queso*
wrapped in tinfoil and a bottle of Peñafiel tangerine soda,
such provision a gift from her son, a picnic

J'ai besoin d'une bon-bon pour mes petits-enfants, vous savez? she
shouts

returns with Hersheys gratefully accepting a crumpled dollar
bill of unknown denomination in return

surprised how easy a city was

but the wounds of this world difficult even to think of

cybercafe in Mombasa at the end of Ramadan, *Tous les sites
Sun glasses avec rugby-engine.com*, tourists in baseball caps come
down from the Grand Regency Hotel ogle the Idd il Fitr
festival, the poet and her lover sowing seeds, *walu i mbo, Wa-
fahamu?*, game of Bao, understand?

have lost the epic sensibility but not its scope

sow the seeds but no longer know the rhythm of sowing

I do not wish to tell a story which begins "a warrior once went out upon the plain"

she does not wish to tell a story

(at the touch of her hand, lets a seed drop from his grasp)

Mekatilili wa Menza, mother of all, Abra in Wittig's *Les Guérillères* with Florelle and 50,000 women archers marching out against Lisuart of Greece

who (Shelton transl., 1612, 1620) more virtuous, more valiant than Amadis de Gaul; more discreet than Palmerin of England; more affable and free than Tirante the White; more gallant than Lisuart of Greece; more comely or more courteous than Rogero, from whom the Dukes of Ferrara at this day are descended, according to Turpin in his Cosmography? All these knights-errant, the very light and glory of knighthood. These, or such as these, are they I wish for

a tad too educated, the poet's lover says

the tea is sweet

c'est pas la gloire

the slow afternoon of being in love

the slow afternoon of being in bed

smiles (Bergman, 1955)

gather their papers, set the board aright, one seed kept later
cast in the gutter: may an orchard grow and shade the beast
of burden (Rolling Stones, 1978), may sweet fruit make the
child smile

nuzzles against his nipple, suckles as he moans

"poetry in motion" (giggle like children)

a pretty, pretty, pretty, pretty, pretty, pretty girl

come on baby please, please, please

"For Lucy, in Hadar 3.75 million years ago / Great Mother
of Us All / For Lake Turkana in Kenya / where it all began"
the American black poet, Lovelace, began her poem

in the jade sea my lover floats, *mbo* swaying like a reed / ibis
dip and feed from his *maziwa*

"girled me," he

she

(whispers) yes, poetic license

post-colonial othering, gender migration, and global trans-
gendering (first launched by Laura deG___, now managed
by Tess with help from Sheriann and Laura)

was

where it began

where it will not end

in the windows of the microbuses and *matatu* tourists' eyes
dull in the glaring heat, sweat between their weary loins,
damp centers, rubbing eyes and foreheads, their fingers
stained with red dust

it is so much better, also damp, to sleep under a white sheet
and then go out into the night and the festival

musical fizz when she pads to the bathroom next to their
shuttered nest

this woman pisses poetry, I swear (her laughter echoes from
the tiled room where she squats)

your hissing like buffalo milk in an old woman's tin pail (she
makes him laugh)

beyond the white shutters the green tree snake drapes in
sleep

in Dubai two birds of paradise in a tall vase, *lalique manqué*,
XVA gallery, proprietress Khan of the New Jersey Khans

we are seeking the real city, Air France captain suavely explains (in English)

nous cherchons la vraie ville

comme tout le monde (his companion, a Lebanese businesswoman and archangel, rejoins)

imperial laughter of the afternoon, black burkas window-shopping at Fendi, narrow hips swaying underneath, club boys laughing at the Mercato Starbucks

steers them to Bastakiya (*l'art de la vie a la xva*) thence to Abra landing

returning instead to an air conditioned hotel bar (El Malecon) in Jumeira

Saffanah, this her city (viz., the foregone Al Fahidi Fort exhibit)

Pierre, sur cette, je construirai, etcetera

archbishop, archangel, not what they seem, Y-chromosomal Adam & mitochondrial Eve, (viz., Pascal *Pensée 83* "the senses mislead the Reason" etc and also ibn Haitham *La Pensée de l'Islam*, Istanbul, 1953, "on the perception of darkness, distance, position, body, size, proportion, appearances, and beauty")

IVF, GIFT, ZIFT, TET, TESE, PGD, ICSI

TAGCCTATAATACAAATTCCAACCCACCTCATCT
GGGGCTT

having come here (Conceive Clinic, PO Box 67, Dubai, UAE, Tel: (97-14) yyy xxxx) too weary for a real world or to sleep

CNN on large screen plasma TV, pearl divers (*saffanah*) view of the universe

. source   1..1888
                /organism="Homo sapiens"
                /chromosome="19"
                /map="19q12-q13.2"
                /cell_type="fibroblasts"

    gene   1..1888
                /gene="PEPD"

ftz spz dnc fkh hh eag

fushi tarazu spätzle dunce / forkhead hedgehog / ether-a-go-go

consider the poor fruit fly (*jubilate agno*)

for having done duty and received blessing he begins to consider himself

is it too much to simply want you inside me?

wife and partner, themselves lovers, pressing lidless eyes and waiting for a knock (TSE), all modern life algebraic, functions and variables *dans une vraie ville, nous établirons un nouveau monde*

what goes on under the moon does not concern the dawn (Persian proverb)

the emir's tent is his own and so too is the silversmith's (purportedly Sufi)

tadpoles (transparent) lash their tails, aswim in a petri dish

fake green glass of minibar coca cola, Larry King goggle-eyes the sound turned down, flesh still damp under crisp 600 TC Egyptian cotton Frette sheets, blue shadows flashing against the gold tapestry wallpaper, hot wiry hair at her center nuzzling against his round buttocks, mmmm, she hums them to sleep

mmmm mmmm (weeping) mmmmmmmm

children all gone, little Ann below the warming pan

augate, augate, envol'teu, ou les juif viendront t'charcheu!

lavender shadow of the 767 over desert sands

melancholy Prospero, Quinquireme of Ninevah

all references lost

où sommes-nous maintenant?

(where are we now? Paris, of course, we are always in Paris.)

it is hard to keep track of all that happens to us

happens? or occurs to?

she cannot say

on ne dit pas

the loneliness of vowels properly pronounced: *l'on* moaning against one's assertive consonantal claim

à rebours, l'Americaine (she's having coffee with a girlfriend: *attend*) waiting for an airplane

à rebours de quoi? Hélène asks

it is a reasonable question

tu sais, en chaque sens, in every sense: *je compte–, prends–, comprends–, fais tout à rebours*

c'est à rebours du bon sens to love a sailor, *n'est-ce pas?*

Hélène likes the American girl's dramatic flair, the present tense sense of victimhood like a silk scarf wound loosely around her slender neck

à nous la liberté, a noose

do you ever look into the sky and imagine him there, gold braids at his cuffs, starched white shirt tucked over the buffed belly, hovering like an angel

comment on dit second-hand?

comme the clock or *les marché aux puces?*

the flea market

trotteuse

trotteuse d'une globe-trotter, je suis, damaged goods *tu compris*

Hélène thought the girl may have meant to say *tu comprends,* but *tout compri*s would do as well, damaged dame *dommage*

her charmed French *à tout point de vue ("en chaque sens," comme elle dit)*

she cannot help but laugh, *la meduse*

that's your lot, she tells the girl *tout compris,* bed and breakfast, *n'est-ce pas?*

L'Americaine laughs *aussi*

do you want his baby / he doesn't want mine

ce n'est pas what I asked, *dit Madame l'avocate*

nor he, *dit elle*

check / mate

it is a political question for him

the spilling of seed always is, Onan's sin the denial of his brother's legacy not the glistening spunk

do you never stop thinking? l'Americaine pleads earnestly, doe-eyed

she supposes not although in thrall they, too, betimes (vide: Proverbs 5:19 "as a loving hind and a pleasant doe, let her breasts satisfy thee at all times") have lain awake thoughtlessly together, and so she knows better, cf. Ruth and young Naomi

"you're right next to me but I need an airplane"

Naomi plays the jukebox in Dalian (Tori Amos), elsewhere in the bright cybercafé Chinese hipsters croon melancholy tunes, it's late at night and no one loves her

China all the way to New York / maybe you got lost in Mexico / you're right next to me

an earnest young man, Ken, Qin Jiang, begs the teacher to explain this

Letras de canciones de Tori Amos—Little Earthquakes—China: search engine hit on the CRT, screen yellow with the smoke of cigarettes and dumplings irony of a yellow screen (she would not mention)

it's algebra she says

Qin drinks Mountain Dew Code Red, a land beyond ironies

Home, I've come home / But not to the home of my longing (she recites)

at first they thought her mad, now they know, Korean American, the picture of her white mother and father beaming, China now used to this: export industry surplus, the words her students favor

Even today when I climb alone / to the end of the mountain, / White-flecked flowers warmly smile (continues)

"How are these song like alber ga?"

how *is* / *this* song / al-*juh*-bra

yes, thank you teacher, thank you thank you

two thanks sufficient except when you sleep together on a first date, it's algebra (laughs)

crazy, his eyes say, also immodest

not a song a poem of Chong Chi-yong, she explains, Korean

unnecessary to footnote this, Chinese can hear it, like Jimmy
Bob, esp. this close to the border (Dalian, very clean, Dan-
dong okay, Sinuiju Korea very dirty, American no go there)

Korean / American

(is Na Oh Mee Korean name?)

crazy

in Hwagae-myeon, Hadong-gun, South Gyeongsang Prov-
ince (Korea) the annual Mountain Dew Tea Cultural Festival
takes places each May

I think it is really about heroin, she says

China, she says

Qin Jiang awaits wisdom

who was Daniel Ansel? she asks

Wikipedia: "colloquially referred to as junk, babania, horse,
golden brown, smack, black tar, big H, lady H, dope, skag,
juice, diesel, daniel ansel's straight potion etc.)"

china white, tea is marijuana

viz., the herbal, (2737 B.C.) of Pen T'sao Ching attributed to
Shen Nung, emperor and herbalist

Ken (Qin) feels he is failing the test

would you sleep with me she would ask but he would report her (the subjunctive)

skinny ass surely skinny yellow cock like a dog, surely he would whimper as her lips surround him

never slept with an Asian save herself

Hebrew = delightful / Japanese = above all, beauty

korea dirty china clean

Na-young the name of a famous Korean actress

Ken drifts away to a video game (*Heiankyo Alien* by Denki Onkyo), excusing, bowing, pardoning, bidding this would-be Barbie, mail order baby, goodbye

outside an old man in a diaper squats beside a blanket selling melon slices, retro Russian whores in satin cruise You-hao Square (Omara Portuondo waltzing with herself, Buena Vista)

Polo Bar Casablanca Cafe Hollywood Cafe Noah's Ark Dalian Club Sizuku (Korean)

so alone (viz., *Hime-chan no Ribon*: Daichi left Hime-chan on his bed (note: she's still in small form) and went to play soccer with Shintaro)

29 year old Man 24 year old Woman Looking for Men,
Women, Couples (man and woman) or Groups Living in
Ulaanbaatar, Mongolia, Mongolia (Friend Finder)

disappearing into the (dou^6, dei^6) d-d-d-dirt

I am going to tell you what happened, eh? Bobbie gets it into
his head to go out in a girl's dress over Doc Martens 8-eye
Union Jack toe cap black high boots on the second day of the
Stampede, promenading through the pancake breakfast with
a white Smithbuilt on his head, and everyone is laughing and
giving him the high sign or the finger, eh, but all in good
spirits, when out of nowhere this weekend cowboy sticks him
once in the gut with a shiv and runs away through the crowd,
people running after him, leaving Bobbie clutching himself
and looking embarrassed about how the blood's spreading
through his fingers and across the belly of his chemise like a
dark crimson azalea. RCMP guy comes back winded from
running but with the cowboy in cuffs and asks, is this him?
Bobbie cannot say by then so they roll him away on a gurney
and into the back of the ambulance taking him to hospital,
but just when they're closing the doors this girl jumps in saying she's his wife and plops down in the jumpseat next to
him, and when he gets out two days later after observation
they move in together, just like that; she's the sticker's by now
ex-girlfriend, see, and she tells Bobbie the way she sees it is
she owes him her love because of what her boyfriend has
done, and they live with each other for three years like that
until she has a baby, then they get married and have two
more kids, and she still tells him how sexy he looked that
morning in that dress and with the garnet feather on his hat
and how the scar is like a ruby under the skin of his gut

don't bullshit me

that's how it was, Old Man he don't want to repeat his mistakes, see, how the Niitsitapi story goes, like once before when the chief of the women took him by the hand he pulled back and broke away and so had to become a tree, always caving down the bank and making him mad

(in another story these same two build a mountain so they can get to the sky and be with their children but in the process the people got mixed up until they came to have many different languages)

another pint, bud (Big Rock)

the inverse of summer, Flames about to come on the television

away game the rangers at the garden (creation myth)

time's a funny thing, mate, eh? ever think how many people are fucking at any one moment in a ten block vicinity

why ten? / the decimal system (self evidently)

five finger annie (laughs)

love her square root

two fools minus one, cowboys in winter without a woman

they cling together, long after they have lapsed, Adèle et Yves, in a third floor apartment just off 9th avenue in Inglewood, cozy in the sleeping loft designed as "equally well for sex, stargazing and sleep," according to the Lifestyles section of *The Sun* which featured the two of them, fully dressed, atop the "viscofoam padded, sturdy faux-silk upholstered platform with panoramic skylight" in their recently renovated apartment, "the flagship space for one of the latest projects in 'Alberta Mainstreets' remarkable renaissance"

Calgary's Hottest Architectural Duo Do It (and we do mean "it"!) Together (headline)

what they discuss (warm air rising from the highly efficient Handöl 10 GT Swedish wood-burning stove with soapstone plinth) is how sad it makes them to be less in love than they were once

he traces the delicate tracery of her aureole, she nuzzles against the hand and licks delicately (once) along his slim index finger, giving him back his hand (and, of course, lifting the weight of it from her small breast)

they know they are comic figures, they earnestly wish to be otherwise

the nipple has tightened involuntarily, the glans of his detumescent penis seems violet in the morning light (later they will go to the gym together)

it is not that I could ever live without you

maybe you should work awhile with someone else

you'd like that, wouldn't you? one more jealous fantasy, eh?

(once he thought she fell in love with a garden designer they had subcontracted for a project in Dalhousie and it excited him; she wasn't sure she would call either love)

if not love then what? / laughter maybe

fell into laughter (hurting him "intensely")

in our fathers' day one would have devoted oneself to philanthropy, raising money for the symphony

(they have too much liquidity, they decided once, another Saturday lingering before brunch)

(*The Sun*) Go-go Calgary professional couple establishes center to provide housing for the homeless, battered women and families, and victims of AIDS

the idea to preserve the rich fabric of a changing city while thinking through attractive, clean, low-cost design as a model for municipal projects here and elsewhere

there was nothing wrong with this, nothing insincere about it

I love you so she says

so what (he laughs, unhurt)

sew buttons, eh? (she tweaks his nipple, pinching enough so it hurts)

we should get dressed

we should lie here all day

the irony of this phrase is too obvious

(they have chosen not to have children, thinking it irresponsible to do so)

in our mothers' day we

Gladys (Welch: lame) gamely makes her way along the concrete incline of the riverbank below the floodwall (Portsmouth, Ohio), jogging (glad is), 15 barge tow wheeling round the buoy just below the bridge

mud smell of catfish and diesel penetrated (suffused) by lilacs, delirious honeysuckle steeping in the damp of dusk, pheromones ("the secret of eros" adv.), no one's daughter, she's an imaginary creature, fell in love with a tugboat captain, perhaps this is him (waves to the pilot house but the John M. Rivers does not answer)

Gladys R. Rivers, a good name (nee Gladys Glanyrafon)

the mayor of Bayswater / he has a lovely daughter

she sits on the water...front / and the waves they lap her downy...

some things better unsaid (*daw deigryn i'm llygad wrth wel'd car-tre' nghariad*) what's missing from ch__ch

and the waves lap and lapse as her foot falls

Portuguese deckhand, a lumper, no taller than a swab, dives off abaft and swims ashore to woo her, hair hanging down

Bishoujo Senshi Sailormoon she croons, putting him off as he runs beside her, *lá vai ela, lá vai ela a borboleta no ar*, soft fingers trailing off his brown cheek (how will he ever get back)

she'll fly him back in her beak, mayhaps? (*talvez*, remember she's imaginary)

a winddog, before long he evaporates

and she runs on (viz., Tykwer) through a mother's subjunctive memory, never bedding down lacking a wished-for mattress stuffed with rosebuds like a department store sachet

having outrun time by now has no meaning, neither next nor when, like nettles, clinging to her

first ever free woman: all it takes is this bleak and empty sadness

emptiness will not leave her though she labors and, breathing rhythmically, pushes dark dark within where his flashlight probes

groaning (o my daughter can you sing me a lullybye?) *veddha wanniya-laeto kuveni yakkha vijaya bambara kavi*

at the cost of what

should not have lain down among, should not have been so

languid, *Auge in Auge*, in Wuppertal, pushing the empty stroller at the zoo past various animals, *z.b., Raubkatzen, Tapire, Eisbären*, taking her picture against the rainforest (*Freiflughalle für tropische Vögel*), the air a confetti of birds, *Fliegende Diamanten*, flying jewels, according to the fancy color brochure

would have been a cosmonaut, flying now the *alte Dame* (Iron Wyvern), stroller chockablock with holiday *Lebensmittel*, Hans (not solo) holding hands with seine Frau, (no princess) Layla (name courtesy of die Mutter, 1970, at that time an "Agitation Free" groupie *am Inis Reise*, getting it on with John L., nonetheless a Clapton fan)

think to see the filmmaker from the train window (*Ostersonntag Vorabend*) visiting his mother

Das Frühjahr ist uns Vater und Mutter, wer nicht sät, hat dann kein Futter.

spring's our mother and father, if you don't sow you can't fodder

die Mutter (1999) in New York, not much interested in *die Beide* (her&him) on bargain tickets, Williamsburg in Brooklyn, which they walked overhearing secrets of Yiddish streets ("no bad mother, no good death" *Judische Sprichwort*)

feared her with child (*Ich bin nie eine Großmutter, liebchen*)

Ich just wanna dance, *du digst?*

walked over the bridge looking for the city, spent the day with a guy they met in a bar, the evening at a fourth of july party smoking dope and lighting sparklers in a steaming third floor walk-up on Rivington where by midnight half the people were naked, eventually going home with a quiet guy who offered his bed but took it back climbing in with them at four in the morning before Hans kneed him in the balls and they grabbed their clothes and left, Layla crying and still carrying the purple teddy bear a fat girl gave her at the party

now (2005) Easter fires along the banks of the Wupper, glowing gold angels rising into the black night, the stroller stuffed with sausages for breakfast, carrots for *Morchelrahmsuppe*, a small lamb roast, Polish hard candies and Easter flowers, after not hearing from her for years there she was (*die Mutter an der Tür*) mother at the door, weeping at the sight of the stroller, old and dried up lips smeared with ruby lipstick like a whore eating a plum

das leere Grab (and/or) Goethe and the Erkling, *Kinderfresser und Kinderschrecker* (baby-eaters & kid-frighteners, the empty tomb, the barren womb) *nie eine Großmutter, muttchen*: spake the *Tochter*, mother to the woman

crying together in the hallway while he emptied the stroller and took the groceries in, *eine Leidensgeschichte, tausenderlei tausendmal*, a thousand times a thousand things a tale of woe

when he woke they were outside on *der Eisenbalkon* holding each other, all the fires out, Easter sun already in the east (*die Ostern Sonne bereits im Osten*)

Ach Mutter, liebe Mutter, Gib du mir einen Rat / Ach Tochter, liebe Tochter, Das Bündel ist geschnüret, Wir fahren in die Welt!

Ach mother, dear mother, give me some advice / Ach daughter, dear daughter, our bundle is tied and the world calls us nigh

half a world away standing by the bandstand to request Stella by Starlight

what's your name, dear?

whatever you want it to be

mistook for a tune by Hoagy Carmichael (Stardust, a standard)

this one goes out for Savannah (a dinky trio in tuxedos at a historic Roanoke resort hotel, lackadaisical drummer pushing wirebrushes, aimless clarinetist sallow-faced, bandleader plinking at the piano, all very sweet) song a robin sings

waiting for someone, thanks

through years of endless springs

waiting for some thing, some thanks

vaguely waltzing waitresses bus tables, trays on their shoulders, overhead the ceiling painted with the constellations a la Grand Central Station (hereabouts headquarters of the Norfolk & Western Railroad, formerly City Point RR to Hopewell and points south, viz., the siege of Petersburg & bridging the Great Dismal Swamp)

murmur of a brook at evening tide ripples through a nook where lovers hide

history told in ball gowns and roadbeds

arrives in a pink linen suit, blue satin shoes, gloves and pearls, church wear, when shown to the table, ancient wrinkleless nurse's face ebony, that smile

we have become old women together

child, we always were, you the oldest baby I ever knew (that ancient laugh)

Mrs. Julia Colbert of Roanoke, Virginia, widow of a railroad man and church deacon

Miss Jewel of once was

single pearl button against the pulse at the dark wrist, the
pulse syncopating as she peels the gloves back gracefully

child, so good to see you look so healthy

cancer, miss jewel

don't everybody these day?

you?

for me's my ticker don't you know (laughs) nuthin could be
finah than Ann Jina, tiny nitro pill under my tongue makes
me a walking time bomb sometimes girl (laughs again, literally familiar this gleeful raucous barking, heads turning
smiling in the dining room, the band on a smoke break, 100
yards beyond the entrance by statute)

happy mother's day, Julia, I'm glad you could come

happy day to you too, child

infecund Stella centerless several years now, tumor the size
of a honeydew (strange fruit)

life was not easy, Julia, she dare not say (briefly wonders
would the older woman waltz with her, like old times, when
the band comes back)

what do you do these days

read my bible, watch TV and wait

do you ever dance?

black hand upon the back of blue-veined one soft as tissue

still in my heart, child, yes

that's good Miss Jewel, I wanted to know you still dance

have come to a dead end, *un cul de sac*, Baluchi orphans sitting on a curbstone shelling groundnuts, off duty pickpockets, Sardar and Sammo, nomad brother and sister, newly arrived from the colonnades *Place des Vosges, Paris*, working the fringes of the crowd surrounding the tango dancers, the jazz bands, string trios, jugglers, themselves likewise artists: Sammo's beaded dress embossed with mirrors, dark eyes upward imploring shawl cowled and pretty as she tugs at the belt buckles of the male tourists, a majolica bowl in her other hand, pretty little beggar version of the dancing girl of Mohenjo-daro; and Sardar meanwhile noting as the tourists instinctively check their wallets, striking the instant the mark satisfies himself it is intact, Sammo at that exact moment tugging just once more, so insistently the poor fellow is sure he will lose his pants or maybe have his worm of a cock twisted off

Sardar, crying Mama Mama! kisses a lady tourist's hand, pulling it to his breast, gripping it so intensely she has to use

her other hand to try to extricate herself while Sammo emp-
ties her purse

it all happened so quickly

think they were gypsies

may have had a tambourine

a while later rise from the curb walk back to the immigrant
hotel put down ten euros for another day feed the rest of the
groundnuts to the squirrels in the park, maybe walk along
the Seine, buy some orangina from a kiosk, eyes open for
something wanting to be taken

Sardar would like to take a ship to Copenhagen, Sammo
wants to study at Paris VIII, both speak English

for Sardar it is *beggari*, he would like to marry his sister off
and sail away

Sammo keeps a photo from someone's wallet, pretending it
is her American boyfriend

would never hurt anyone, no jail can hold them, slipping
through the cracks like postcards

wanders off from her marching band, Kafka Square Prague,
Wilbur-Clatonia (Nebraska) HS euphonium player Jana Mo-
lachek in red plumed hat and tails and is never seen again,
or so they say

some players read bass clef at concert pitch, others treble clef at B♭ pitch

Jana wants to get away is all, first ditches the dumb plastic hat in a corner trash bin, pulls off the inverted vee-curve crested jacket and garish baldric in a makeshift dressing room behind a saffron Indian print curtain in a shop corner, trading it for a blue gauze summer dress like a cloud (she means the sky, of course), pulls down the satin striped marching pants and rolls them into a bundle stuffing them in the sack that will do for luggage, and at the last minute plucks a straw bonnet from the head of a manikin, pulling its embroidered rim down over her face, and enters the crowd outside the shop where she drowns

imagining a fairy tale wherein she runs away with her glock player boyfriend, likewise a defector, eating sweet buns and living happily ever after like the Nebraska Czech-Slovak Queen

late night dreams turned to desperation, drugged and perhaps raped by a pretty, slit-eyed Russian boy she's met at a pizzeria near the Old Town Square and driven to a Lithuanian brothel where she's kept sedated for weeks, losing thirty-five pounds and never seeing him again

another version wherein she ascends a miraculous stairway appearing in the sky over Prague Castle and there she meets a glass prince (7-Inch G-Spot shaft with multicolored Dichroic inside-out artwork)

or perhaps merely lost when the chaperones find her, stripped
of her dreams and embroidered hat and bound for (a) kitch-
en, (b) laundromat, and (c) community college respectively,
taking classes toward an AAS degree in physical therapy
while her mom watches seven-month-old Ivan

black face of the mummified drowned girl, *Cerne Matky Bozi*,
floating up from the river near the town of Cím, blue dress
billowing in the dank water

heavy damage from high wind and hail reported in several
southern Nebraska counties, including the towns of Firth,
Wilbur, Clatonia and Beatrice, where

late in your century you americans began to feel your story
was less interesting and thus turned to varieties of pornogra-
phy (sips her tea)

Golden Tulip Rainbow Hotel Oslofjord Oslo Conference for
the American Studies Association of Norway

baptized Signe, thus comes by her profession honestly

only a whore comes by her profession, honestly (laughs)

what's in a Signe? / wouldn't you like to know

sat on her rug, biding time, drinking wine

Signe Linn Grønli precisely

isn't it good

"varieties of frontier narrative in video games"

sexy title

Bare hyggelig. you think so? academic equivalent of plain brown oxfords, "ludological lullabies" would a been sexy, like silver running shoes

fleet footed Iris, you're sexy Signe

(so you think, she thinks)

sexy sadie

so Alfred, are you flirting over tea?

"The just man builds on a modest foundation and gradually proceeds to greater things."

who's that? your beloved Possum, no doubt, from his cantos?

Nei, my mother from the cradle, countermanded Afred Magnus the philosopher king

Ohthere, a Norwegian, sailed round North Cape from Halgoland into the Cwen-Sæ, entering the mouth of the river Dvina, his voyage ending at Archangel, the northernmost sea port of mother Russia

vil du ligge med meg i kveld?

what's that?

you need to learn a language (smiles)

do you have a husband

that doesn't matter and it's none of your business, we don't
marry here and anyway my boyfriend doesn't care

post-hermeneutics is

she signals the waiter, *Kan jeg få regningen?*

something about the next session

made a fool of everyone, Sexy Signe

cinema beyond cybernetics Grønli cites Maureen O'Hara in
How Green Was My Valley

Det var hyggelig å treffe deg, Alf. Hade!

Hade, he knows this much.

Ha-ever big you think you are, *hade* Sadie (sadly)

(love a language game) amber pool left in her teacup, oily rim
where her lip

and in a small skiff farther out to sea than it should be a sailor is fucking his girlfriend, her elbows propped upon a thwart, ass upward, knees padded by a folded jibsheet, crying "harder, harder" in English like a porn film, ponytail swaying as she squeals

he's riding the sea as best he can, a lone sea osprey overhead unconcerned, traversing the northern waters

they'll found a new land, salt sea to sweet, *sans ancêtres, ohne Nachkommen*

becalmed begins to weep, salt tears falling on salt lips, on his back rib to rib on the bottom of the boat, she vaguely caressing him, a sea above to match the one that rocks underneath

baby, baby, she (in English again)

sea sea sea recurs (anthroposophic she)

what is it? (she sea)

moi pentjukh pizdoi nakrylsja

what? (*ch`to?*)

my mind's gone out of whack

poor baby fucked silly, *tu compris*?

oui (we)

below here used to be a valley, a village, hills, lanes, wandering cattle, a whole world under the sea

to what purpose? he (in English)

what's the meaning of life, you mean? (she laughs and plucks idly where his root nests hidden from the sun between his legs, plump as a sea cucumber)

mon tokamak, she (whispering) "are you familiar with the hairy ball theory?"

quotha lady physicist to her fisherman

"one cannot comb the hair on a ball smooth"

feeling a rousing there

(eye eee, she, i.e., *id est*) no nonvanishing continuous tangent vector field exists on a sphere.

piz`dyulina (strokes her pubic hair)

dampening sea

pizdato, she moans, *poide'm popizdim* (presses against him)

again? you're insatiable, my ass will be red as a baboon

pizdetc (it's our fate) she whispers, the boat rocking again under the invisible moon

still he wonders, becalmed, sea cleft, lost

kak pozhivaesh'? / *zaebis*

(fuck 'til you're blue in the face / then what)

shadow of a cloud on the water lapses over them like the hand of god

unpenetrated (unrepentant) we've made a turn toward home, Rembrandt streets *de Amsterdamse Jordaan*

thus domestic keyboard sounds, kitchen clamor and humming

(Chomolangma blog): at North Col, 7000 m descended to 5400 in order to acclimatize

can you get away long enough to eat you think

some frostbite in the face but expects it to heal with some skin lotion, still early in the season

arm slung round her aproned waist, mmmmm, *Kaeng som phak bung phrik sod kab pla* and crispy fried noodle (*Mee Krob*)

me crab you jane

(kisses) you handsome me gretel

you do / so much

each make soup or pasta or something simple every other day, make love twice or thrice weekly, alternate laundry sundays, walk down to the canal bank some evenings, hand in hand, what's not to like of such a life

monitor the high slopes, care for herbs, look out for one another and neighbors

the sherpas have put up tents at 8300 m from Sunday the team will start forcing to new heights, first to Advance Base Camp at 6400, then to 7000 and farther to 8000.

thereafter will descend to 6400 in order to recuperate for 11 days

so much we do meaningless

a recipe but repeated gestures

we could be anywhere

yet gestures fasten us

can see the summit. It keeps snowing there, and the summit is often covered in dark clouds.

want what we

on the satellite radio, as if a soundtrack, the Dutchman
falls asleep and Margaret blows the candle out,

what we want we

cannot say

plan now to make the first attempt to reach the summit on

which then a better question, how long we've been together
or the longest we've been apart

when I look at you it's as if a mirror

flex time + disembodiment

"Ash-a! Ash-a!" Cf. Skt. *A'SA* or *AS*, "ashes"

a shiva song we sing we all fall

finding herself confused the reverend andrea bunshaft, of
Pond Inlet NU (Mittimatalik, Nunavut) reflects before her
service at the Grise Fiord outstation church St. Peter's

been thinking of a phrase as a theme for what she would
preach:

we know all we do not know

(alt: we do not know all we know)

she could not say now, headachy from the cold and feeling
lonely again for daughter and grandchildren

betimes captured by inversions like singsong, inside out the
same, a seam

god's northernmost edge a husband's cold flank, conjugal
deathbed

wing dipping into the turn and with it her stomach also turning

and what, pray, reverend father mother, what ye sister powers and spirits, would be the antonym of Milton's nethermost
abyss? this upmost apex, this blinding light, this searing shelf
of ice, say you, the largest Anglican diocese in the world in
terms of area—give or take four million square kilometers,
a third of the land area of Canada, bleak brilliant whiteness
belied at ground level by dog scat, oil spill, spew of entrails,
vomitus

whosoever lives amidst such castings cannot fail to be anything but wise

you see them dialing in on the sermon as if a shortwave
radio, quickly rejecting what is not of interest, the baby jesu
a black fetus tossed on the snow

"I thought God was too holy for me to get close to him"
(quod vide, qv, Annie Tertiluk, Ungava seeress)

we know all we do not know, my Full Gospel Sister

sometimes a brevigraph consists of only the mark, which is itself the
base-line letter (e.g., swash e, ampersand, and other Tironian marks for
con *and* rum*)*

yet (she thinks) a hunter would relate to this could she get it
right: what's known *is* not known, and what's not known *is*
worth knowing = the nature of god

or love (self evident)

vide (but they will not look, too hard to see at this extreme,
yet almost none wearing the Inuit slit goggles of the sort she
fashioned from cardboard as a girl, now even ancients raccoon
eyed, Sedna herself wearing Julbo Arctic Sunglasses, 100%
UV protection+ alti Spectron x6 Polycarbonate lens): Aquinas
"the cloud of unknowing, in which a soul is oned with God"

oned with another, unowned

beata illa mulier, qui sedet in sua domo et sedet post fornacern

called forth from her hearth (Hestia) by an advert quoted in
Go Forth: "nine priests sought for arctic parishes"

the muses number amusing her daughter, how obvious can
you be, go forth no less

didn't want to lose her, didn't want to be lost, the charter
bouncing on updrafts, the landing strip like a tongue, smoke
rising straight up from the Co-op

why mother, why?

sent Guajiro song via email by way of partial answer (Re:
Why? WHy? Why!? via Michel Perrin):

we, the shamans, eat tobacco and sing
the spirits sing through our mouths
you can't understand them, no one knows that language
it's like a telephone that is attached to our heads

still in the snow at the edge of dreams an image of the fiery-
haired granddaughter, Grace, as aptly named as her grandmother isn't

backwash of gasoline faintly through the cockpit vent

spirit of God, descend upon my heart, she prayed with Croly
and Augustine, bringing the plane in, hummed to herself
the healing hymn of Hildegard, *O ignis spiritus paracliti, de te*
nubes fluunt, ether volat, through you clouds flow and ether takes
wing, *de te lapides humorem habent*, through you even stones grow
moist, *O spiraculum sanctitatis*, teach me to feel that thou art, *O*
dulcis gustus in pectoribus, winged goddess, teach me to feel

alone on Vashon island, the gardener considers the banded
wood snail, *Cepaea nemoralis* (Linnaeus, 1758)

damp form cupped in his palm, the plump glans retracting

our reading today from the Book of Enoch:

heliciform; opaque, not very glossy; brightly colored varie-
gated (brown, orange, yellow) with blackish or cocoa spiral
bands sometimes coalesced or absent; whorls convex; pe-
riphery rounded; suture deep; last whorl strongly descending
at the lip; protoconch smooth; teleoconch with axial striae
and wrinkles; aperture wider than high without and den-
ticles within; columella slightly thickened and usually dark
coloured; basal lip thickened, straight and not evenly curved
into the outer and columellar lips; outer lip moderately thickened and slightly recurved; umbilicus absent

pseudepigraphic apocalypse midst Asiatic lilies and Hima-
layan honeysuckle. the Enochian walks with God (as a god)
along a path of pea gravel

Jane Lead's (1694) root which fed with Balsamic Virtue the
Rosie Flower of the Mind; its beauty of a Blushing freshness
always put forth, now appearing fortnightly for a Microsoft
exec

yet each evening crawls forth the indomitable Grovesnail
while across Elliot Bay forget-me-not pulses through side-
walk cracks along Capitol Hill, and here scarlet cup fungus
(*Sarcoscypha coccinea*) brims with rainwater atop a nurse log
along the margin of the red cedars

life cannot be stopped (and yet you have no children?)

lives alone here god on his island only occasionally troubled
by this pleasantly descending couple who claim never to pre-
sume to own that which put forth itself

"A Flower from the Paradisiacal ground hath appeared, the Nature and Property of which is never to fade, or die"

earnestly at intervals his apparent employer attempts to explain what he calls his philosophy, i.e., we are all caretakers at a different level of granularity…no one ever really owns the code, at least not once it's out there…the net shows us that the world's all flow (they have houses on Kauai, in Montana, Connecticut and in the Juras near Besançon whence came her family)

"An Experimental Account of what was Known, Seen, and Met withal there"

otherwise known as ecstasy (and yet you do not love?)

blue-leaved *Rosa glauca* need little pruning, still today Jared will work among them, stepping carefully among plantings of smokebush, meadow rue, and blue oat grass

helicopter plock & thwack announces the Olympians' arrival (and yet he does not move, no one's servant, more like Caliban than a god)

every day he thinks he should go to the city

sketches delicate veins of the dusky violet *Cardamine pratensis*, a difficultly procured Cruciferae from the summit of Gold Mount in the Jura with which he has yet to surprise her

fond of the damp, she and this flower both

the cellphone camera to "capture" (so it says) the drawing (to document what? and yet sends it to no one?)

after a brown bottle of sweet stout homebrew brought for lunch (a good bait for snails as well), naps, a satyr, shirtless in the sun upon an empty altar, as if the goddess might discover him there

in the seaside town of Karlskrona, Sweden (SE), a former naval fortress with a hidden city beneath its streets, two trombone virtuosi, six foot tall blond valkyrie, Karin and Mimi Petersson Hammar, sisters, their quintet known as Sliding Hammers, play Jobim's *Chega de Saudade* slowly to an appreciative audience at Jazzklubb Cupol

badly translated as "No More Blues" this tune was recorded by Joe Henderson on *Double Rainbow: Music of Antonio Carlos Jobim*, Polygram #27222, March 21, 1995 with Herbie Hancock on piano, most everybody agreeing Herbie in this cut stealing the show

none of that shit matters, man, Joe he's a god, righteous motor city freeform bebop saxman

Chega de saudade, a realidade é que sem ela não há paz: "The time of my haunts is measured by 'saudade'—the samba feeling." Ulmer's reverent phrase (viz., Keller, T. "Preaching in a Postmodern City," *the movement: Global City Church Planting*, ezine, June 2004) not a translation yet could be

*Não há beleza, é só tristeza e a melancolia que não sai de mim, Não sai
de mim, não sai*

No beauty, only sadness and a melancholy that never leaves
me, never leaves me, never leaves

aquavit, for instance

discography ≠ theology

sway the sisters smiling each, eyes blue as gin on ice

Lars Erik S., professor of theology at Uppsala University
(faculty of Studies in Faith and Ideologies) and the American
cybertheorist, Anna M., of the Georgia Institute of Technol-
ogy, thrown into each other's company during a conference
on the global city, sit with a group of Swedish doctoral students watching the Hammar sisters intently, heads swaying
dreamily

adverbial life

tomorrow the two have been promised a tour of the hidden
city

founded by papal bull (Sixtus IV 1477) Uppsala's perhaps
most famous figures (the ubiquity of Professor Celsius' legacy notwithstanding) being Strindberg and Linnaeus; "it's like
two sides of a coin," Lars Erik says during a pensive passage
of the samba, and the jazz-dazed graduate students glance
harshly his way but dare not say anything given his rank

the American nods vigorously making the three silver rings that stud her lips jiggle slightly, a fourth ring, thick like a chain link, lifts her left eyebrow while the right ear is armored with a ring of piercings, twenty silver hoops before he loses count

not looking away from the Sliding Hammers, Anna M. brushes black spiky hair back from her pale face (on her bicep the tattoo of an ideogram she thinks to mean serenity)

two characters (she explains to those who ask): a woman safe under the roof of her house

not coming on to her or anything, he thinks wearily, just attempting to be friendly

"the privileges of 1593 marked the great turning," he continues to whisper in her girded ear, "to be sure three of the seven professorial chairs established were in Theology; but of the other four, three were in Astronomy, Physics and Latin eloquence, do you see?"

nods but to what, the music or him, unknown, agnostic, grooving (serenity)

looks up to see the taller Hammar sister (Karin?) staring out at him, humming to herself whilst the bassist takes his solo, her benign, even kind eyes holding him and her hips swaying gently in the dark waves, then taking up the trombone once more with a small smile leaving him alone again and washed in doubt earlier leaving the conference in sharp, icy rain Anna M. had told him about an essay by Hubert Dreyfus called "Kierkegaard on the Information Highway"; beginning, she said, with an extended quote from Dylan's "Highway 61 Revisited"

seeming to believe Kierkegaard was Swedish

as a gift exchange for this citation Lars Erik offered an antique description of the very city where they stood, a charming and more comforting vision of the place lit by warm memories, a promise of the storm's aftermath from *The Wonderful Adventures of Nils.* (*Nils Holgerssons underbara resa genom Sverige* 1906) by Selma Lagerlöf (Nobel laureate whose face, he showed Anna—digging in his pocket to find a 20 Kronor note—engraved in violet ink, a half-smile under a huge bonnet)

this children's book, for decades a required school text, his daughter Frida had loved, both in Swedish and, later once she learned English, in translation, a book he had read more times perhaps than the scriptures:

It was a moonlight evening in Karlskrona—calm and beautiful. But earlier in the day, there had been rain and wind; and the people must have thought that the bad weather still continued, for hardly a soul had ventured out into the streets.

While the city lay there so desolate, Akka, the wild goose, and her flock, came flying toward it over Vemmön and Pantarholmen. They were out in the late evening to seek a sleeping place on the islands. They couldn't remain inland because they were disturbed by Smirre Fox wherever they lighted.

you see, he said, they feel safe on the outside

nodding Anna M. pulled up the hood of her anorak

you memorized all this?

not memorized but lived it, he mused, already feeling foolish, vaguely longing to see Frida who studied now in South
Africa

*tentationes secum habent dubitationem de praesentia et misericordia
Domini* Swedenborg wrote (a kind of a samba) in the *Arcana
Coelestia*

a thousand telephones that don't ring, tell me where I can get
rid of these things (not a translation yet could be)

laughing the graduate students headed off with Anna M.
along sleet silver streets, Lars Erik off alone in the opposite
direction, pleading fatigue and the need to be home, spotted
Smirre Fox near the car park slipping away furtively up an
alley, eyes gleaming like a cat's, the alien theologian left in
fear and trembling, coaxing his Volvo awake

Angie wishes there were more of these tales with the names
of things, weather, and the inner thoughts of characters
(would be a reason to have children she supposes)

instead reads her devotional texts and ordinance manuals

the search for god is endless, Elvis having left the theatre laughs over stale tea, orphan and eremite she

lives nowhere (or beyond description)

I used to discuss with my brother ways and means of becoming martyrs, and we agreed to go together to the land of the Moors, begging our way for the love of God, so that we might be beheaded there. I believe that our Lord had given us courage enough even at that tender age, if only we could have seen a way. But our parents seemed to us a very great hindrance. (Teresa of Avila, saint)

PFC Angela Louise Paolucci, C Co, TF 1-18, 2 BCT, 1st ID ("The Big Red One") FOB DANGER (formerly Camp Ironhorse) sits in the unrelieving shade of what was once a (hometown) presidential compound, one of many such jewels strewn in this desert

Tikrit, someone said when they first came here, means "the Gate of Hell is fully open" but later a translator said it really means "At the End of the World Waiting for Utopia is Finished"

"Either way the scum cunt of the world," a sergeant joked (then added, "Pardon my Farsi, private ma'am.").

"For the fitness fanatic, the palace gym has a full weight room with stationary bikes and punching bags and offers 'Thai boxing' classes every Thursday night at 1900 and step aerobics and kickboxing classes Monday, Wednesday and Friday at 0600. Fitness aside, the MWR has a sports bar, an internet cafe and a movie theater. The sports bar features two big screen televisions, billiards tables, a bar stocked with snacks and beverages, and a 'Music Night' every Friday, Saturday and Sunday from 1930-0100."

irregularly scheduled "indirect fire attacks" commence nightly

glory of god likewise descending intermittently in tongues of fire

O my God, what must a soul be like when it is in ecstasy! Longing to be all one tongue with which to praise the Lord. (Avila)

having her period again, again out of cycle

to reach something good it is very useful to have gone astray, and thus acquire experience (Avila)

fingering the effigy of *La Madonna della Grotta* (vicinity Praia a Mare, Italian Riviera) pressed into Angie's hand when they shipped out by her Calabrian grandmother also Angela, of Newark, New Jersey

è il grembo della terra, the old woman insisted, *il ventre della terra*

che cosa è grembo, nonna?

Utero, ventre, figa? (points to her belly, impatient, a girl should know)

figa, she did know, a bad word, the cunt in its excess and lusciousness a fig to boys (bloody now)

womb of the earth, karst cave carved from the flank of Mount
Vinciolo, evidences stratified human settlements from Upper
Palaeolithic, Mesolithic and even the Neolithic periods

desert effigy of the sea goddess, venerated alike by Muslims
out of respect for the mother of a prophet (Jesus) as well as
their respect for Fatima, the Prophet Mohammed's daughter

none of it matters, she is nowhere, without any details (two
statues: *della grotta* wooden from 14th century and *della Neve*
marble 17th century)

the fig of the world cramping

pain is never permanent (Avila)

mystic in the sun, they want to murder her

the lady of Fatima appeared to the Portuguese children,
Lucia, Francisco, and Jacinta, at *no Cova de Iria*, commonly
called the Cove of Peace, though more properly the womb
of the world (i.e., the cove of what will be)

having killed no one, slept with none, tortured no one, loved
none, laughed with few, nor yet been wounded, raped, beat-
en, or otherwise assaulted (has however seen the eyes of the
dead, both the zombies and the sleepers, those who yet walk
this earth and those who rest in sandalwood boxes but whose
names she increasingly cannot remember)

still / born

our body has this defect that, the more it is provided care and comforts, the more needs and desires it finds. (Avila)

the sun beats down again in the old tales, viz., the story of Saint Zita

Torniamo a Zita che gia` cresciut'era, con gran pensiero di servire Iddio

time passed and the girl grew, happy enough to do god's work, or so they say

ma dove è dio? she wondered, then went in to look for ice

oval river stones (seven)

wabi, tabi, shibui, koko, yugen and seijaku the latter she explains "the state of things seen by the eye of an ordinary person" such as *fuka* (weathering), *shinbaku* (erosion), and *mematsu* (wear) (cf. Dr. Koichi Kawana)

it doesn't add up (do not get it)

is what is unsaid

what?

no need to designate anything beyond the river and the form of the stones, for instance but there is no garden

we are stardust (trivia question: *Click here to send Eva Cassidy polyphonic ringtone to your cell phone*)

unregenerate hippie

99 Divisadero 1974, white kitchen with 6-ft tall cabinets

"the 'element of time'" (ibid, i.e., Kawana, his quotation marks)

billowing dress with no curves, *miroir sans image*, or bare feet

laving the smooth stones with a river of buttermilk (shiva lingum), meant to induce lichen growth

2 March *Maha Shivarati* (the holiest night of the year)

reads: "paste of all the parts—flower, fruit, leaves and root—smeared on the phallus two hours before the actual intercourse and wiped out clean just before the intercourse. The woman experiences extreme excitement during such intercourse."

they laugh

each? or as one?

mirror with no image

West 98th St. 1969 NYC alone in a single white room "penthouse," little more than a shack on a brownstone roof steaming tarpaper beach outside its back door, painted walls, ceiling, and floor, the whole cube, with white lacquer, within it one blue (Danish) sleeper sofa, one Parsons table (painted black), two spoons, two knives, two forks (Dansk), two leaded crystal water tumblers, stereo bolted to the floor after the burglary, exactly 32 books

Noah of the inanimate, Moses calendar (a month plus one)

monkish to her nunnish, a desert father

her litany (Miranda):

mother hen, Mother Hubbard, Mother Jones, Mother liquor, mother lode, Mother Nature, mother of thyme, Mother of vinegar, mother tongue, mother wit, Mother Superior, mother's boy, mother's daughter, Mother's Day, Mother's mark, mother's milk, Mother Meera, Mother Nature, Mother Night, Mother Of All Bombs, Mother of God, Mother of Israel, Mother of pearl, Mother of the House, Mother of Us All, Mother Redcap, Mother Russia, Mother Seton, Mother Shipton, Mother Svea, Mother Teresa, Mother West Wind, mother wit, mother yaw, mother water

neither foolish nor wise but have survived into simplicity

how did you find me?

delectable said the cannibal king (Shri Badat of Gilgit, a Buddhist) crooning

And every night by the pale moonlight
you'll hear him say
Ba doom
Ba doom
Ba dee ya dee yeah

no (seriously) really?

diligent through cities, mendicant disguised as a window shopper, poking solitary midst the tatter of railroad yards and warehouse margins, outlying homeless camps of foraged construction site plywood in the deep brush along the Harlem River; other times seeking channel to channel through infomercials for resurrection, body fat melting away in just ten days, face transformed by herbal secret of the ancients and genetic engineering, youthful complexion revived by this miracle preparation (*fuka, shinbaku, mematsu*)

have something now

nothing is what we have, "the element of time" a possession outside economy, nor place nor names (bombers not turning into butterflies, *Las monarcas no soportan las bajas temperaturas y caen congeladas sobre la nieve en el refugio El Rosarió, Michoacán*)

hibernation: jewels congealed in snow

stone garden tranquility (the word smooth)

hope never snuffed as long as you lived it (uncertainly, awkward, distant, unbeknownst) on my behalf for you water tasted of stone whilst for me it was the contrary, the sifted dust flowing in rivulets and pooling, a rush of streams the willows bent to drink, air thick with tiny insects like golden pinpoints, manna upon the grass, gilt children running gleefully through a metallic mist, quotidian magic

the petrol bomber™ in the mural at the Free Derry Corner after a decade thankfully has ceased whispering incessantly to Sárá from behind his monstrous mask

glee frighted, or the laugh that is a scream, contorted, tortured, whisper

make him stop she

was once

still lingers in memory the sickly smell of the CS gas perversely reminiscent of Críostóir's rough scent ("old space" he called it, always a joker) long years ago

Bridey, the boy insisted upon calling her, child's voice raspy with blistering because the masks fail to seal completely, *Bridey help me Bridey*

cradling his petrol canister like a wee doll wide eyed behind the malign comic proboscis

she could do nothing, nothing what she could do

Bridey help me: transcribed in Pittman shorthand, a sound the hand the eye recognize, *a (bat), e (bet), i (bit) I (eye) oi (boy)*

plugging ears with waxed cotton sometimes to snuff his awful pleading

Bridey Bridey please

Críostóir, a Mayo man thusly likewise a baptizer, spake her name sweetly (erstly), the Gaelic way at first and thence his sing-song naughty English: "Ach Sorchan, my shining one, my Sally, shag all my darling but your snow white feet…"

Óra a Sorchan, a Sorchan Ní Bhruinnealla, A chuisle is a stóirín, éalaigh is imigh liom.

baptizer, blatherer, blaguer, altering the lyrics to suit her

Óra, Sárá, Sárá Ní Bhruinnealla, My heart's beloved, elope and come along with me.

shag all shinings Petrol boy and Mayo man took from

"A para near to a 3 tonne lorry on Rossville Street threatened the boy with a pistol and shouted at him to stop. Another para then approached the boy but before he got to him a third para came up behind him and hit him with his rifle butt. The boy said 'God don't hit me!'"

Saolaítear na daoine uile saor agus comionann ina ndínit agus ina gcearta.

"all that is human born free and equal in dignity and rights"

coming out of the dark, viz., the abyss of Kildare, St. Bride (b. ca 450), a Druid, daughter of Dubhthach, court poet (*fili*) to King Loeghaire.

Bridey help me, let us pray

Deliver us, Lord, from an inordinate love of this world, that, following the example of thy servant Bridget, we may serve thee with singleness of heart

(rest the soul of Daniel Hegarty and those who died in places where the circumstances do not permit a commemorative)

Simon Fisher asking (symposium @ INCORE two scant months after the American towers fell) can a Fijian, a North American and a Colombian learn the same lesson?

can an Irishman, Bridey

please

help us mother, come over here, you can retire and just be their dear *Seanmhathair*

nana

okay. Nana. *Tá mé go breá.* It's all the same.

university Irish, Cleveland Heights gaeltecht, *iníon* infatuated with her fathertongue

dissolves the distance, language does, resurrection of the dead

Nuala & Cathal morphing through a series of email jpegs, grandchildren growing older, IM-ing

sd 2 her u wrk 4 peace, mum, peas? she sd, yuk!

from Gk. *stenos* "narrow" (of unknown origin) + *graphos* "writing," first recorded 1809

Pittman gone the way of Erse

NB. This transcript was typed from a transcription unit recording and not copied from an original script. Because of the possibility of mishearing, INCORE cannot vouch for it's complete accuracy.

a wld 2 remake

2jours will B

won't ever B 4 me

my pt xactly!

(empty)

Slán go fóill, mom

Slán leat, iníon

xxxooxxx

Paku's grandfather Tjipto's having ceased to be a pirate, dozes now in retirement on the beach Buyat Bay while off-shore the scientific ship takes core samples

the fish have gone away, the water spoiled by mine tailings, even household cats gone crazy

twenty of them that day boarded the Alondra Rainbow outside of Kuala Tanjung (1999), ten in the fast boat, Tjipto among them, ten more joining after they captured the ship and tied up the master and his crew

Paku wants to know how it was, imagines Disney DVD, X marks the spot, pirate map, John Depp and mainsails billowing

the second ten remain in the Mumbai penitentiary, Tjipto and his comrades turning back in the speedboat after offloading the crew and half the aluminum ingots to the second tanker, fast boat guys top label, cream of the crop, AK-47 and percussion grenades, no knife but still plenty *Silat*, thank you (the Alondra Rainbow repainted and bound for Fujeira, Saudi Arabia when intercepted by the Indian navy)

would be his last time out

Please, *kakek*? Paku pleads

"Sudah makan banyak garam, adik, sudah bijaksana." Tjipto de-
clares, enough salt makes wisdom, a sailor's saying (gesturing
lazily toward the bay) there, the future is there, the scientific boat, go to university, Institut Teknologi Bandung, study
oceanography, *mendayung antara dua karang*, steer between the
rocks, drink Johnnie Walker Black, not kill your brain with
Arak

Tuak + Coke = Paku's drink

"habis manis sepah dibuang," Tjipto mutters, "when it's no longer sweet, throw it away"

he means everything

adik believes nothing of course, it is the way of the world, he
wants an iPod, halfway believes his grandfather could swim
out and snatch him one from the science ship

Tjipto lights a Marlboro but refuses to give the boy one so
Paku pulls out his own pack of Djurum and lights one, the
clove smell good to the old man and so they trade

not so old really but three bullets still in his wiry body, knife
scars on one cheek and both arms, bone fragments floating
in his swollen knee years now since it was crushed by a crow-
bar, shooting the face off the mate who swung it, another
time *Nyi Roro Kidul*, the sea goddess, pulling him by his hair
from the depths of the sea just as he had drowned and was
walking the streets of heaven squinting at the radiant light

Sorgaloka

there is no heaven, here is heaven

upon a mat of Medong grass on a dead beach Tjipto re-
clines, Paku squatting beside and studying the horizon, their
smoke intertwining on the breezeless afternoon

Ayahku adalah pensiunan pegawai negri, my dad's a retired civil
servant, Puku's mother tells neighbors

true enough, *Menurut cerita orang-orang, banyak perompak bermu-
kim di Sukarno,* even the president surrounded by pirates

the boy waits, with the fish gone even the birds have left, all
that remains of the future now *omong kosong* (empty talk)

"Tapi, sore esoknya aku sudah lagi..." Tjipto sighs (there again
late in the day)

the old pirate dreams of Kebon Manggu, garden of man-
goes, *Sorgaloka*, paradise

Nyi Roro Kidul fragrant as ylang-ylang when she pulled him
from the sea, her soft breasts against his shoulder as she
swam

on a high stool at the circulation desk the American surveys
god's creation, former Jesuit, Desert Father *sine prole supersite*,
i.e., without issue

that somewhere in the reeds a child is born to change the world
struck the librarian, irreligious otherwise, as extraordinary

despite the cliché his true religion, frankly, categorization, the rightness of things, e.g., "If the distance between eternity and non-eternity is greater than that between the various species, how then is it possible to apply a judgment about the opposite extremes of the empirical world and the invisible?" (Ibn Rushd known as Averroé)

ethics (and aesthetics) indexical: what belongs where, and how it is (re)called

drawn to this desert city as much seeking the distinction between Averroé's *ayat muhkamat* and *ayat mutashabihat*—the unambiguous and its contrary—as he was (to the dismay of his family and, respectively, the Society of Jesus and of Friends) out of devotion to good works

not unconscious that the former pursuit perhaps subsumes the latter

12/13/01 "wayward Israeli rocket" strikes Ramallah Friends School

terrorism or self-defense

9 mos post secondary school library position interview @ RFS turned back after detention and questioning Ben Gurion airport, Tel Aviv, flew back to Indiana to await reentry

the reeds and the water, for instance, flow and potentiality, the basket snagged on a cattail, all history in the balance staying the assassin's arm

re the passage (Qur'an 3,7) where obscure, elegant argu-
ments turn on the thorn of a comma, a breathstop really,
dotted rest: *waqfa lazim* at a crucial (from Fr. *crucial*, ligaments
of the knee via L. *crux* "cross," viz., *Instantias Crucis*, Francis
Bacon,1620, X'ed signposts of a road fork = must choose)

"no one knows its hidden meanings except God" (here the
waqfa lazim) "and those who are firmly grounded in knowledge they say: 'We believe in it, the whole of it is from our
Lord...'"

hanging in its eddy whether only god can know or wise men
also can

the children come and go seeking books on superheroes
(Arafat or Batman), the librarian speaks only English, inutile
Latin, passing French (of Arabic not much more than the
internet's joking "four essential phrases for every traveler":
wein odati, wein al-shat, wein al-bar, ma timsikni hunak (Where is
my room?—the beach?—the bar? Don't touch me there!)

imperial premises of a tourist class no joking matter

Lif Yassar, Lif Yameen, Ala Tool, Shway Shway (go left, go right,
straight ahead, slowly slowly)

straight & narrow versus?

Alf Layla wa Layla (1001 nights)

was

"God does not think other things as being other than himself but as identical with his essence" (*Talkhis Kitab al-Jadal*, commentary on Aristotle's logic)

fruit of the vine and work of human hands

Jewish sewage flowing along the so-called separation wall will eventually feed Palestinian orange groves, Moses rafting on a river of shit

lotus

*Fasl al-Maqal fi ma bayn al-Shari`a wa al-hikma min al-Ittisal*, Decisive Treatise on the Harmony between Philosophy and Religious Law (Shari`a)

"a prison of culture" someone in the news said of Ramallah

film festival audience in tears laughing at *Rana's Wedding, Jerusalem Another Day*, in which not wanting to leave for Egypt with her father Rana sneaks from their house at daybreak and wanders through East Jerusalem and Ramallah looking for her boyfriend.

alone in the audience the librarian spots a handsome young woman he knows, Palestinian lawyer, older sister to one of the RFS students, Mariam, her smile and smooth brown arms enough reason to sign on another year he thinks

al-Kulliyyat (Book of Medicine from Aristotle's Universals,1153-69) comprises seven books: *Tashrih al-a'lda'* (anatomy of organs), *al-Sihha* (on wellbeing) *al-Marad* (on illness), *al-'Alamat* (of symptoms), *al-Adwiya wa 'l-aghdhiya* (of things taken by mouth) *Hifz al-sihha* (on cleanthliness), and *Shifa al-amrad* (on treatment)

after the festival screening retracing Rana's steps through Ramallah streets stops for coffee at Kanbata Zaman ("once a shoe store") Café

everything used to be something but how to love he wonders

lines up tamarind seeds Chowrunghee compound Kolkata the girl named Ishya Aamani (diviner twice casting names meaning spring! miracle of Namkaran Sanskar that prompts a poojah in thanks to Mother Lakshmi)

her parents call her princess

shuunyha, ek, do, tiin, chaar, paanch, chhe, saath, aaTh, nau

looks up in satisfaction

the nanny (a British girl) applauds but then gently moves the girl back more deeply into shade

"one, two, three, four, please"

lining up seeds again *shuunyha, ek, do, tiin*

in Kali Ghat a little goddess scatters seeds and again lines them up

whether teach her the *Chintha gilla atta* game or simply amuse
herself Millicent cannot say

the gurgle of iced Guruji Rose Sharbat from the thermos
brings the princess running, in her place a kingfisher descends rooting for insects among the scattered seeds

hooting, she chases it away, rubies splashing from the drink

the bird rising lazily, upward in slow circles

in the panchatantra tale the bird Sindhuka's droppings turning to gold, do you know it? Ishya Kumari?

(English, speak English! her employers insist)

the girl laughs: my mother is not me

not your own daughter you mean

confused diminutives

well of dark eyes gazing upward

Ishya devi then, Millicent says, settling it

sweetly the girl awaits the story, cross-legged at the young
woman's feet

tomorrow the princess will fly away to Los Angeles where her
father has a home in the hills and Millicent will go on holiday
to a beach in Thailand

instead of the story she sings a song she learned long ago in first form

I Diwali, I Diwali,
Festival is here today,
I Diwali, I Diwali,
Boys and girls come out to play

I Diwali, I Diwali,
Princess Sita's gone away,
I Diwali, I Diwali,
Monkey's gone to find her,
I Diwali, I Diwali,
Prince is looking all the day.

Ishya Aamani yawns (Millicent, don't you want to be in love?)

patram puspam phalam toyam, whispers in reply, *yo me bhaktya prayacchati*

"a leaf, a flower, a berry, even a drop of water pleases if offered with love"

Ishya devi smiles and sleeps, held in the Gita, safe from the afternoon sun

once upon

African boy eating flatbread skips from state to state at the four corners monument, Navajo Nation, but no one scolds him

she smiles at him (each of them a flirt) and consults the topographic map, her boyfriend looking over her shoulder, the brim of his hat a crescent shadow across her breast and shoulder (each wear Outdoor Research, his Helios in khaki, 50+ UPS rated, her sand color Sun Runner with sun skirt 30+ but big enough for all her hair makes her he says look like a desert nun)

HELOISE (to Abelard): As if you knew one…

Priscilla, Queen of the Desert, he thinks

Processo de Cartas de Amores, "Process of Maps of Loves" (Venice, 1553), translated as *La complainte et avis, que fait Luzindaro prince d'Ethiopie e l'encontre d'amour, et une dame*, "Lament and Opinion of Luzindaro, Prince of Ethiopia, After an Encounter with Love and a Lady" (Antwerp, 1561)

headed for Three Corn pueblito in Dinetah, ancestral Navajo land not far from Four Corners they'll have to climb the rock to where it sits and she's a little worried

sheen of perspiration makes small pearls midst wisps of blond upon her upper lip

nuzzles "Don't!" she protests and snatches the map away with the kiss

does not like being upside down, neither on a rock face nor a roller coaster or face down on a pillow in a bed?

how can you be so horny in this heat?

wanna head for Glacier National Park instead?

it's a long walk, better wank off in a restroom stall

again? (she laughs and swats him with the map of the progress of love)

African family slides into a silver Escalade SUV with dark shaded glass, mother in a white robe with long shawl gathered round head and shoulders disappearing into darkness, the man in a snakeskin green silk pajama suit and gold embroidered matching cap, the boy wearing Nikes and a Monument Valley tee shirt looking back as the door closes

better to think of the pueblito as a space station than a sacred outpost, the trek there neither encouraged nor discouraged, the thirteen rooms scheduled for "ruins stabilization," not even a pebble the Navajo park ranger said, "don't come away with nothing but dust on your feet and…" (grins behind mirror glasses) "whatever the spirits whisper in your ear."

making it sound dirty

ranger came upon them at Old Fort, 1st century AD (circa Apollonius of Tyana) to Three Corn 18th Century (circa Samuel Johnson), kept looking at her tee shirt, innocent enough, a kid, pumps iron climb dangerous, she asked

not for a good body, *ahdzah'nih*

when the Ranger left she asked Troy whether her nipples were showing

yes, he said, pulling the shirt up over her face and brim of her sunhat, leaving her blind and exposed to the spirit world

bastard! echo of her laughter dissipating in the gaps between the stones of the ruined walls

(from the guidebook) *the afterbirth is offered to a young Juniper or Pinon, the tree and the child thereafter growing together in a sacred bond throughout their lives, thus the cradleboard made of the same wood, a gift of the Holy People, in the long boards embodies a child's mother, the earth, and its father, the sun, in the cross boards. A blanket of clouds with ties of lightning holds the child fast while above its head, a shade bent like a rainbow keeps it safe*

coolness in these ancient walls she runs her hands over

vaguely sexual stirring

as if stones could give suckle (how the sun felt on her that moment)

huge stone knob at Three Corn a blockish carbuncle at first like so much of Monument Valley but with an aspect of an airship (space on her mind) the ruins atop the mesa like the cabin of an upturned zeppelin if stones could fly

they do, we call them comets

and planets

climb not perilous as much as wearing (Trailbook: *Three Corn is a 13 room ruin constructed during the Gubernador era. Access is very difficult and requires gymnastic skills*) by the end of the hike not just nipples but all else soaked and traced through sweaty shirt and shorts and with no one else there except the spirits took her clothes off and set them out to dry, rubbing her body with cornstarch where she chafed, walking the stone floors in bare feet until she found a place where they could make love comfortably insisting on taking him in in the old way, thighs spread to cradle him, staring upward to the blue of the cloudless sky from the shade of the wall where they lay within a world's eye older than any enlightenment

far far above sharp glint of some high aircraft turning in the sun surveilling both them and every part of sacred creation, yellow hawk and locust off in pursuit, chasing the intruder to the dome of the world, she following after as she came, thumb pressing the seed into the damp soil and seals it, *hozho*, all creation briefly in balance, like a feather on a breeze, kernel of her daughter already growing in her womb soft tendril of corn sprouting forth

was a good world to be one who could find water

imagine the sky a plastic sheet held down at the sides by banks of earth, he tells her, a pebble dropped there at its center like a nipple will direct the condensate to a container placed at the low point where it sags beneath it

dampness even in the desert (shyly)

what he did was he drilled for water learning how from his father whose father's father's father learned from an Wang-kangurru mikiri-digger whose people already knew a thousand years ago how to angle a bore through Simpson Desert sand reaching water bearing layers

no son yet to teach it

desert earth to him like sky to others yet still left the Never Never as soon as he was able, setting off from Birdville and not stopping until the Southern Ocean and stayed there happy as a yabby in sweet water

back then only well driller's licence a strong hand and nose for oil or water, flamin' Department of Water, Land and Biodiversity Conservation not yet in play, i.e., licence and permit required of any who "wish to construct a well to a depth of more that 2.5 metres (or if working on a well at this depth) anywhere in South Australia"

innythin' less than that's a bathtub (laughs to himself)

buggered in a boozer, near sixty year old bore even to him

Cannuwaukina Bore water rises hot as from a billy on the stove

amazing facts of the well driller

and you expect to find a wife like you dig for water?

his Gawler Place in the mirror not half bad really, blue eye and green eye, still no awning over the toy shop, clean, even tempered, frugal, big bikkies in the bank, drill rig and ute both fully paid-for

and the incentive for a woman of child-bearing age to root with such a codger?

careful hands, soft for a driller, generous spirit, longevity: dad still kicking at 95, his father before him dying peacefully at 88, great-grandfather married his third wife, age 19, at 63 gave her a baby at the first scrum

knowledge of dampness goes without saying

childless young widow Evangeline stone farmhouse near Springton still right enough if she'd take on an aging bogan could keep her in the style accustomed

bore pumped at 3,000 gph @1725 ppm, holding dam gravity fed toilet and stock troughs, 16,000 gallon rainwater to house plus underground tank, maybe 20,000 gallons

Vangy's man fell from a horse two years before and died in a sec, now seems a happy little Vegemite, lonely like she didn't want him to go

and the color of her eyes?

he'll have a pint, yes bless you, tongue as dry as a nun's nasty

but it really happened, do you see? (leering cobber in the mirror beyond the bar is him) lingered that first day and drank sweet water together, since then rang her ten times on the Al Capone (documented by scratchmarks on the parlour wall) leaving a message each time on the machine, Vangy calling back eleven times, at the last invitation driving the ute out there tonight, bottle of Old Block under the seat (won't drink a plonk called Dry Bore thanks)

the secret to be a talker, a woman loves that, and a man, if he's honest, wants to be

have kiddie winks together if she wants and live forever until the end

ofttimes in a cellar you can smell the water under, "yam who I yam," Popeye sez to Olive Oyl, Jehovah likewise to the Jews

the explosion was deafening as they say

iron rose opening to a moment without beginning or end, Dijana picking flowers for her mama woke without leg and mother both in the clinic at Gorazde, whispering help me, *povredila...povredila sam se* no one hearing her, not even herself

pretty petals turning to fireworks sound louder than thunder bursting her ears

meni treba doctor, povredila sam se, povredila sam se

life began then, she thinks, held the flower of creation and watched the world turn inside out

sounds of it coming back in circles

curious sad eyes of the little girl on the cot next to her, Medrima, like black olives on a plate

izgubila sam torbu, her plaintive whisper made Medrima laugh at first until the coughing tore her broken ribs, screaming, the wide eyes unmoving as if it wasn't her

a comic error

izgubila sam torbu, I've lost my bag, for *izgubila sam noga*, I've lost my leg

cvjetati, flowers, attempting to explain to the girl who was screaming placidly as if a strange song, too tired to say more disappeared into an endless meadow, waking to find them sisters by circumstance

fallen from a cherry tree the orphan Medrima put one hand
down on a mine and when the blast threw her back put the
remaining hand on another, a field of possibilities

Dijana's mother running endlessly across the meadow to her
newly orphaned daughter

the new sisters leaving together, beleaguered foreign doctors
hardly paying mind

a decade after now the usual problems: "CheeryBlossoms"
Medrima's blog for instance chokes the Pentium computer
from the charitable trust upon which Dijana's herbal mail
order business, or how after she sleeps the girl and her irreligious boyfriend look at porn together via satellite and laugh,
fuck on the sofa afterward, towel spread beneath them, also
Nena, her grandmother in Visegrad still lives in fear of the
Skorpion paramilitary, and both sisters each still have these
dreams, wishes for love, and and and: the kitchen roof leaks,
next year Medrima will go to university to become a social
worker, the world has forgotten everything, she only hears
through one ear, walks on one leg

tells Miroslav, her organic farmer friend, a computer science
teacher at the Gymnazija, her state in some ways seems no
different to her than that of someone who has lost a great
deal of weight after being obese: as if another version of
oneself continues to exist in another dimension, floating like
an astronaut on a space walk

an alternate universe (Miroslav)

tethered by memory to the mother ship, she whispers, not certain whether he can hear her

it does not matter, for lunch they have a salad of watercress and edible flowers he's brought her

of those happy alone necessarily no one speaks

logically so

or by definition

an interesting distinction logic v. definition

thing you must watch for, extending internal dialogue beyond what the situation warrants, else become a public spectacle

with cellular telephones, however, the antisocial and schizo-phrenic less distinguishable

research says a dog or cat can help with this, but then you have to tolerate the filth of an animal

when we used to smoke corktips where did we suppose the stubs went? who, looking at the puff of a kitten in a pet shop window, thinks of shit

nor is one ever told what to do with a dead body

what do others think and how does time pass for them

how was it Heidegger put it

"fucking Nazis" his nephew would mutter each time they came upon trekkers with collapsible walking sticks

charming (and charmed) intolerance of young men

we have not yet we have not

am no one to most people, more and more perhaps even to me

still in search of and so

how did the old riddle go? brothers and sisters none his own father and son

around the middle of the building a continuous ribbon of light, stories updated every minute repeat themselves at two minute intervals all the same

happy? amen. so be it tra la

those old couples you see watching traffic

not yet begun to think

cannot remember pain they say or any scent, say new mown grass or garden soil

nos habebit humus in due time so now rejoice etcetera

what wonders

greeting card computer chip plays the motif of Minuet in F
No 3 for Anna Magdalena Bach when opened, for instance

re / wind

regarding the wind she thinks

errors and wrecks cannot make us cohere

mother in a chair mother in a chair mother in a chair mother
in a chair mother in a chair motherinachair motherinachair-
motherinachair (her mother, this old woman, chants, child
happy mother in a chair)

she's complained that she's not happy her

here? you mean

no answer

and how do you think one feels seeing her mother in a chair

"her," she blurts (almost attribute it to mischief rather than
disease)

would rather mischief

speaking as if reading

in her purse a five inch by two inch electronic translator with
28 languages including phonetic hebrew, arabic, chinese,
japanese, korean, thai, and indonesian over 580,000 words
(20,000 per language) and 58,000 useful phrases, 8 currency
conversions and 6 metric conversions, world time in 200 cities and calculator on 2 line x 14 character LCD display

also a discreet ivory pocket rocket with travel case, tin of
mints, handful of bite-sized Baby Ruth bars which her mother dotes on in her dotage

smiles

having fun, are you? mother in a chair inquires, chewing
paper and all and so have to wrest it from her, start again

well yes she supposes if this is what is left to us

True Light Home for the Aged, Hong Kong, without a word
of Chinese beyond 28 characters at a time

mother an old china hand china hand china hand after a
decade working for the telco, what Cantonese she mutters
now not in the pocket machine

we are your forever family now. *Jin hou, wo men jiu shi ni yong
yuan de jia.*

arrows for the rising, flat, and falling tones, dash for the flat,
check for the rising falling

ma (rising) *ma / dang* (flat) mother chair

what is your name? *lei giu me ye meng?*

don't be foolish, Celia, (chewing the wrapper again) I'm your mother

Celia was your mother, mom, I'm Beth your daughter

nei yui hui bin? where are you going? *nei ju hai bin?* where do you live?

neither something settled upon nor something that has happened to us, nor are you not you any less than this is who you are, my distant star, my mother

knows who is whom, can recall clearly, crisply, the name of her nurse, Anna (rising tone) she calls her, An Sheng, old fashioned nurse cap and uniform like a 40's movie

yes missus

entering the waypoints of their girl's gravesite (-34.059, 24.8775) outside Humansdorp where they live on and she now lies, eTrex® Venture® GPS, its green translucent case like a spaceship

no other space on earth having these numbers, anyone coming from elsewhere able to find her, no longer splayed upsidedown in the bus, no longer pale and oddly smiling upon the hospital slab, no longer rose powdered in a satin lined box before weeping chums

beyond this cemetery slope the world's largest man is bur-
ied, not far from here the fynbos floral kingdom extends for
kilometers, not far Big Tree, Fallen Tree and Table Mountain, not far either Kouga the domed place of dreaming
where 120,000 years ago human beings emerged from the
bush

seventeen years on this earth

none sharing the location of this space wherein his child lies,
sun bronzed ivory flanks back to ivory at the end, laughing
her netball teammates said when the bus went over the N1
south of Bloemfontein

of the 39 only three chosen for this honor

gone mad he wondered how it was to make your way along
this dim path as she did, where none could be summoned
to explain or witness or console, where what one saw could
never be reported; it made him proud of her, his daughter, as
proud as seeing her rush on wing attack full flight to the very
edge of the shooting circle

each realm open now, each circle of heaven and hell

kept thinking absurdly that this accomplishment brought her
(sweetJennie) into the company of John Lennon and Brenda
Fassie

celebrity of death's commonplace coordinates

went crazy really is what he'll say when they ask how did you stand this (none will ask, nor he be able to explain, neither witness nor consolation)

despite that panicky interlude years ago schoolgirls scratching each other with shared pins on the playground on a lark after an HIV lecture, nonetheless Pieter sincerely (awkwardly) found himself wondering, even dare he say hoping, perhaps she had lost her virginity before

known love, that is, before

before this what

this accomplishment this event this happened the accident the tragedy this bloody fucking thisness

held in another's arms before disappearing into the earth

like most mothers Marguerite knows all, of course, but he would never ask her, or not now at least, her hand when they lowered the box squeezing his until the wedding ring left a mark on the numb fingers, eyes wide as if she were falling

maudlin really in any case what a father can't know or oughtn't wonder

blubbering rugger Eric Jennie's boyfriend gently touching her cold cheek like some imagined cinema hero, florid and choking in unaccustomed necktie, weeping teammates grappling him like a band of apes in a pantomime of sympathy

how anything is or was, this or any other this

wellspring of monthly blood, sweet salt taste of lips and face, slow motion screams and tumbling, distant shouting, bus turtled up engine still running

this last kiss

(shows Marguerite the screen and explains) these coordinates you see mark the center of the grave, longitude and latitude of where the stone will be, where she, so to speak, forever will be

can you enter her age there, perhaps make it blink? shall we make a web page? Marguerite asks unfairly, tears welling like distant rain

O Pieter what has happened to us

nothing and everything

held numb in each other

there used to be a heaven

stille waters diepe grond, onder dwaal die duiwels rond

deep waters run mild but devils wander underneath

caught in a riptide years ago swimming off of Paradise Beach at Jeffrey's Bay saw Marguerite and Jennie happily waving to him as if a dream, the little girl's hand in hers, wind too strong to shout what was happening, eyes burning with salt mist, heart pounding, no one around to help, and, swimming parallel to the beach until the ocean released him, stumbled finally to shore, ragged arms too weary to lift up the by-then utterly frightened girl

Voilà la fromagere! vierge numéro onze mille et un

makes her way slowly with her sheep, Our Lady of Langlade, the eleven thousandth and first virgin of Sainte Pierre and environs, cheesemaker, ex-chanteuse, fallen woman

literally, not fallen in some Paris salon like Violetta but rather stumbling upon a mossy rock (*Addio del passato*) in pursuit of her woeful and bedraggled flock, Marie Antoinette of the Onze Myll Virgines Archipelago in workboots and jeans

recuperant now making her first (re)appearance *sur la coteau*, Mme _____ (*nom de guerre* now *sous rature* instead call her ex) formerly a principal at l'Opéra de Montréal now appearing nightly last bastion *de l'empire français* (*les deux d'entre eux dans la retraite*, she and the islands, *les deux retitré*, both done for, both renamed if not renewed)

solfeggio de la do re mi (sings)

Fais do do, Frasquita mon petit frere
Fais do do, t'auras du lolo

La Esmeralda Emagaldua, with apologies to Goring Thomas
et alia, "Oh, vision entrancing!" Frasquita, the little Basque
sheepdog, yelps happily, their first postlapsarian promenade

emagaldua, fr. Basque "lost woman," (*littéralement*) now "bitch"
as in *vous etes* / you are: "*Zure ama emagaldua da*"

rebaptizing herself not Esmé but *Ederne*, Basque for beauty
(eternity a false friend as they say) dipping a cramped hand
into cold Atlantic waters

choosing vanity above esteem (though who will see this wild
woman, she wonders, save the boatman)

and of course *le médecin de la salle d'urgence*

fully Francophone Montrealer, opera house Italian and
Deutsch, her Basque before this limited however to Guridi's
lovely Zarzuela trifle, *El caserío* (*Amaya* never interesting her,
nor ever likely to have been offered)

resumé of living alone includes—not to mention current
pastoral life—three decades so spent before footlights and
wandering rues of the Plateau arm in arm with beaus of all
sexes like the diva she was

usual complement of lovers, promoters, and hangers-on
(laughs)

Frasquita yelps, wind whips in from the ocean, the sheep
complaining

climbing a corkscrew road one night through the Laurentians toward Mount Tremblant en route to the so-called cottage of one of the aforementioned lovers and hangers-on, *soi-disant* former industrialist styling himself a composer of sorts having made a fortune inventing a synthesizer circuit or something, weekend supply of Veuve Cliquot in a cooler, passing through one of the procession of gaudy dreary provincial towns, i.e., Ste. Adele, Ste. Agathe, Ste. Quelquechose, etcetera, spotting a skinny table dancer smoking a cigarette under the blue lights of a parking lot outside a topless club, the sequins of her teddy blue as the lights, nicely shaped long legs under fishnet stockings but otherwise a homely girl, garish bow lips below a cyanide punk hairdo and freakishly painted eyes, nonetheless at least for this moment feeling herself filled with a longing to be like the dancer in the deserted parking lot, free for now, watching a solitary car wind its way up the mountain, evening air and menthol smoke chilling her lungs before she goes back in

sisters of mercy sweetening the night without and within

man with the car and the cottage, the Quebecois composer, went by the name Michael not Michel, Anglophone archangel manqué, one of a series, wanted to be married to someone, thought she might be her

for some reason a magnetic attraction to that name—two Michels, a Miguel and three (*oui, trois!*) full-fledged Michaels counting this one over the years—not all by any means angels, nonetheless an ironic history in common with her present island, Basque baptizing it après several Mikes, fishermen so

named and early on established here, Micquetõ then Mic-
quelle over time giving way to Miclon, Micklon, and the pre-
sentday Miquelon

Sainte Pierre (*sur cette roche je construirai* etc) less interesting and
who in the world would one tell all this to in any case

she, too, giving way over time (yet never married, *merci*)

Oi zer bakea!… Harriak ere mintzo dira! (Basque saying) *Oh! quelle
paix!…meme les pierres l'affirment, ou*

such peace even the stones affirm it

(still they try to break you)

free now before the sea

whole of tomorrow morning (*Fais do do, t'auras du lolo*) to
be spent shipping internet orders for *son fromage fait maison*,
Miquelon Ederne, "dense, semi-firm texture with delicate
aromatic herbaceaousness, a tang of seacoast salinity and
rich, buttery finish"

now appearing on the best tables in North America and Eu-
rope

braving the wind, facing east, Frasquita yapping at her feet

brava, cara! encore brava, bakea!

the words run through the head of the half-awake sailor

who will be your lover, lover

qué será, he thinks (disappointment as a kid finding it meant
what the line that follows said)

wishing language were a knot?

music anyways

Doris Mayday

Q: name a revolutionary starlet

hums across short waves

(viz., Van Morrison, days before and so on)

apprec info re Perry James & The Rumours "Who will be
your lover tonight?"

qué será

inbox only pharmaceutical spam + porn, sailing under a
moonless sky, taconite to the loadline, two hours before sun-
rise (@5:22 AM CDT) bound from Superior to Gary, grab-
bing twenty minutes to himself proofing bread and sweet
rolls before putting them in the oven

man without a country

Cliff Robertson made 4 TV or poor Paki bastard living in the Paris airport (cf. stowaway teen frozen in 757 wheelwell)

PUBLIC PROFILE

Gender: Male

Interested in Meeting People for: Friends, Activity Partners

Status:

Age:

Occupation: steward (cook)

Location: f4r fr0m fr13nd5 4nd h0m3

leet=far away

light gaining, buttery perfume of turnovers

w15h1n6 | 4n6u463 w3r3 4 kn07

incomparable pleasure of sailing in fair weather toward the dawn, even the wheelsman lingering in the pilothouse after midwatch the eastward light unfurling

$1.556302500767287 \ x\cos^{-1} 58=$

Musa refuses the crayons the Human Rights Watch doctor gives the other children of the refugee camp, keeping a vigilant eye lest his sister return and he miss her, otherwise not wanting to see anything ever again

90.26554504450266 √

thought a pocket calculator from a knapsack would perhaps keep the boy distracted

9.500818125009165 x684013.2=

the old, the weak, the blind rounded up and shot, the people still hiding in their huts, Janjaweed, Sudan soldier, and planes and bombs, men in green are taking the women and the girls forcing them to be wife, pushing pushing hitting

64997281.98135645

screaming running to hide in the *wadi*, holding each other by the arms to keep together

7.777777777777778e+23=

numerals' dim march across the narrow horizon seems at first to soothe him

6.049382716049383e+47

conjures her smiling, Sara there among the glyphs on the screen

infinity sideways 8

if we could be together I would be so happy

darigi jugi, (putting down the toy) please mister I need to go
back home

99999999999999999999999999999

snow candles along the far ridge of the valley, *Otaru Yuki
Akari-no Michi* transported to Forcella del Fargno along the
road from Pintura di Bolognola

gold miracle of mountains glowing beneath banks of white

for the dead chrysanthemums, for the living christmas cac-
tus

dusky lavender folds below San Marino, down in the valley
below the darkening hill distant fireworks of a village Feste
de l'Unità like children's sparklers, forlorn brass band tune
drifting upward, drifts of laughter and earnest communist
tarantella

Sagra del Coniglio Serra San Quirico

celebration of roast meat, *sugu, salsiccia*

rabbit and spider cursed, lovers moving off into the darkness,
bottles of chilled sangiovese like Italian ices age 9 Niagara
Street Buffalo NY

procession of empty saints nonetheless what salvation we
have

in each swail or hollow someone's story, legs spread, what fullness there is

"volontieri parlerei a quei due che 'nsieme vanno, e paion sì al vento esser leggeri" (would love to speak with those two the wind carries so lightly—Inferno, Canto V)

august dreams dry february stars frozen white, july smell of first hay in january, jewels rising from the dull chaff: lapis locusts

moan of love in a dry time

we die we die

for love (or chocolate, he grunts)

late in a slow time the single not easily known (vide the-extinct-great auk, CO)

poets will not come again

invisible lattice of mist across the valley manna of information descending from satellites like tiny angels on parachutes, the smoke from bonfires of razor sharp canes twining with incense of olive prunings, fireflies rising

we grow up many

but can't we please just stop awhile and hear something all the way through

J'ai acheté un écran plat (proudly, dateline: Le Cap)

Cap-Haïtien autrefois Cap-Français "Paris of the Antilles."

Grete Sultan's sprightly precise Goldberg Variations on the Platine Verdier Turntable, fingering clear as ice, a longing beneath unlike Gould's

pale yellow spinnaker of a sailboat on Manzanillo Bay, ten stories below some sort of riot aborts their plan to drive out to Limonade and witness the exodus of vaudou societies for the Feast of St. Anne

DVD of Bresson's B&W *Au Hasard Balthazar* plays in silence upon Leveret's new plasma screen where the small Gauguin had hung

rum poured over tumblers of ice and lime slices

our hopes sunk, he says, *Noël en juillet, n'est pas?*

how so Christmas in July?

singsong of rum

voilá, laissez-moi expliquent

little fishing village called Bord de Mer de Limonade at the end of a dirt road where the Santa Maria sank Christmas day 1492 *the* Santa Maria?

exactement, de Colombus, aucun autres,

and with it our hopes

Leveret's affronted, *rien ne descend nos espoirs, mon ami*

but you said! *mais tu as dit* Stephen does not say

a friendship fastened over innumerable coffees Swarthmore Village in the 90's, especially after *la mort du père de Leveret,* the true lion of *la Compagnie Café Leonce* Leveret now heads

Limonade tout était si infini, tu sais?

Cixous essay read together in a feminist ethics class, 199x, two lacrosse players, *frères* among the girls with full breasts and unshaven legs

Koteki gin amou, Leveret says in creole, where there is love, *n'est-ce pas*

Stephen supposes

et pour toi, he says, *où est l'amour*

Leveret laughs

dans le disco de l'hôtel de Mont Joli where the rebels headquarter now, *maintenant il y a de nulle part*

whether he means the disease or the rebellion Stephen can
not say

making all his nowhere plans *pour personne*

Date: Fri, 27 Jun 2003 10:43:33 -0400
To: Daedalus <svg@xxxx.com>
From: Bunny < Leveret@CaféLeonce.fr >
Subject: mother dying come home father
Cc:
Bcc:
X-Attachments:

cher S

cocktails have lost their kick, "mere Combivit doesn't thrill me at all,"
(C. Porter) not long, je crains (je crois) for the new (or any) world,
descendez please *et bid adieu*

grosses bises!

Bunny

in summer sun on the platform at Pula an old Croat woman in
dimija and headscarf and American Teva sandals with faded
blue floral straps has seized the only shade at this end of the
platform pressing close to the fence under what looks like a
chokeberry tree the branches nearly touching her head while
bees move in and out of the leaves nectaring on the tattered

blossoms occasionally alighting on her scarf and hair before she swats them away; ducking to extract a candy from a cloth handbag at her feet brings an increase of bees drawn by the scent of sweetness, hovering before her and veering by turns toward her face; slowly she opens her lips as if to sing and one by one bees dart in and out of the shadow of her mouth as she stands there unmoving; the train to Ljubljana arrives and so he is not able to witness the dénouement if any

tresses of Signora Svevo (Livia) in the photograph at the museum in Trieste were he wrote "long and reddish blond" (cf. Courbet's portrait of Johanna Huffington, "Jo, *La Belle Irlandaise*," mistress of Whistler painted at Trouville now hanging at the Metropolitan Museum in New York); and the Liffey he went on "passes dye-houses and its waters are reddish so I've enjoyed comparing these two things in the book I'm writing"

obvious connection likewise to the melissae of Maha Devi (Kundalini) who manifests herself in a sound form, queen bee surrounded by the hive, Bhramari Devi "awakening in a buzz of ascending consciousness and descending spiritual grace" or so says Layne Redmond, the drummer (surname, of course, from the German, *rote mund*, "red mouth"), whose tresses in the website publicity pix likewise long and reddish

do   you   see   how   it   is

via Ljubljana to Rijeka or Zagreb, or, if you wish, back to Trieste

as the succession of present moments displaces former pas-
sions, *a tutti avviene di ricordarsi con piú fervore del passato quando il
presente acquista un'importanza maggiore*, (La Coscienza di Zeno,
cap. 5) even Svevo's famous Christmas roses fading

handsome black man in the window seat studiously reading a
book called *Does God Believe in You: Developing Spiritual Self-Con-
fidence* as they break through the overcast into brilliant blue,
sunlight bronzing his delicate fingers like a silk handkerchief
and she cannot help laughing

yet he seems to take no note of her

elsewhere however goggle-eyed god of the blue looking up
comically from the seatback, tiki face of upturned (emptied)
sample size vodka bottles five dollars each, makes her giggle
and then, embarrassingly, burp complimentary grapefruit
juice

sweet scent of alcohol and citrus

without looking up from his book pushes the flight attendant
call button

yes please

can you ask this woman not to disturb me?

she and she exchanging glances

there has been some misunderstanding

pardon me sir

(one of them says this)

she's drunk I think, she will not listen

you never tried

are you two traveling together

no (each say simultaneously, ought to hook pinkies she thinks, feeling almost crazy giddy dares not giggle lest proving his point before the manicured SAS flight attendant sternly leaning over their seats like a judge)

absurd she says he's making it all up

struggles to recall the tai chi sequence called white lotus (quigong form)

Goddess Presents a Peach followed by Eight Celestial Beings Drunkenness, then Golden Lotus Dancing, and Fragrance Blows Over Earth

not for the life of her able to remember which movement comes after these and before Goddess Flying and Fairy Maiden Spreads Out Flowers (whispers to herself: Wuji, Tàijí, Mabu, already feeling the calm)

yet now not exactly the moment to stand up in the aisle and work through the form in proprioceptive memory

Buddha's Light Shines Over Everywhere she knows is followed by Crossing a River in Heaven

I am sorry if I disturbed you

the two handmaidens await the divine master's reply

(no, she thinks, await kindly, without anger or irony)

he continues to read

from the attendant, as if by rote, a peroration

sir, this aircraft is filled to capacity but if you like I could ask if anyone would exchange seats with you; these seats are too close, people lose patience

the latter offered to nearby rows as well by way of a general opining

a clash of civilizations and beliefs, she cannot stop herself from blurting and the flight attendant, thrown off script, bursts out laughing

it is wrong, she knows, they have humiliated him but she, too, laughs

are you a Christian he asks her

I'll leave you two to work this out the flight attendant says, skedaddling still smiling

was she says but I don't go to church

he snorts and goes back to reading

how your mind works crazily as if searching for something to say, recalls a line from *Fear and Trembling* that stayed with her after she wrote a paper about it in college, how the tragic hero makes his life significant by what he does and chatter only weakens it

what she thinks she means is she should have kept her mind to herself

journey telescoping outward like a narrow aluminum cylinder bending softly into a bow under its own weight from point to point across the horizon, arching like the Egyptian sky goddess, Seth or Nut, she could never remember which was which, a long corridor you moved through strapped into your seat like a tunnel of love or something

hypnotic repetition of "it's a small world" Anaheim flume ride makes you want to kill

out of one into another silver corridor at the airport extending into another and another narrowing finally to the vanishing point like when a film irises down to a black dot disappearing

perhaps the angel of death has come to claim her she thinks and, freaked, puts the earphones on falling asleep for the rest of the flight gilded african disappears after passport control at Arlanda and when the bags finally come out of the luggage carousel a procession of them together is followed by an empty expanse and then her bag all alone, as if it had been pulled aside for some reason, this followed by another, longer empty space and another crowd of bags

weird how things happen

demi-plié, plié, plié plus vite tendus dégagés à la première et quatrième pas de cheval rond de jambe a terre frappé fondu rond de jambe en l'air

along the margins of Parque Bolivia, languid and dusty, the iguanas blink like bishops

each morning at the border of the sea walking the earth along El Malecon from Las Peñas, El Ruso's feet likewise dusty, eyes heavy-lidded, sagging under the weight of the light after twenty years as the dance master of Guayaquil

last of the night's coolness disappears into the shadows of the cathedral

El Ruso and the iguana each moving gracefully toward what shade there is

each veterans of constant relocation

his old studio space in the barrio now a tourist boutique crammed with souvenir Galapagos creatures, when *la Condesa* dies his room, too, will be lost earth's royalty passing away in the face of development

all but the lizards in their armor, the tortoises in their vast domes

Vse tam bulem, a piece of the churchyard fits everyone

leathery feet in sandals horned with knobby bunions, gnarled as the creatures of Isla Isabela, face oblanceolate, shaped like a tobacco leaf a whore once told him, even he shocked by the resemblance to a magazine illustration of the Don Quijote Cristo by a Mexican painter, Jesús somebody, though his hair perhaps greyer, face less yellow

a familiar figure even to the thieves and pickpockets who leave him alone on his morning pilgrimage to and from the new studio, nodding to him on evenings when he comes down for the *cantinas* and the *putas*

each morning stopping at the edge of La Plaza de la Independencia for a *Cuáker* from the cart of Doña Carmen, the chilled oatmeal drink restoring the blood, each morning also documenting the dreams of the night previous in a leather bound book of handmade paper, licking the pencil between sentences, crabbed script like code

three women sit discussing lingerie, each dressed quite properly in couture and small hats, various bright tweeds of wool and silk, a sense that this is in Paris although they speak English, their conversation not at all erotic but rather technical, matters of cut and support and fine stitches, the merits of underwires—one laments the disappearance of bone stays;

they pick delicately at unbuttered toast in an antique silver English toast rack, probably Edwardian, kept trying to speak but they took no notice of him, there was a plate of sardines before him, plump flanks viscous with a gunmetal sheen, beside them a gauze-wrapped lemon quarter secured by an azure ribbon

creation in all its variety: in this dust these girded creatures, ancient saints, followed an hour from now by his young dancers climbing the stairs to the studio like postulants, earnest and demure girls in pastel leotards, spawn of bankers and lawyers, offspring of merchants and the better criminal classes, sweetness of perfectly formed calves and breasts in bud, delicacy one dare no longer speak

Mafiocracy posts videos of drugged Czech girls, post-Perestroika empires of porn, two *baklany* even showing up here years ago, tax collectors of a kind, *sborschiki* taking care of a countryman's business in a far-flung empire, the proposal *po ponyatiyam*, understand, an agreement among gentlemen, showing him the webcam

"A tomar por el culo" get fucked up the ass, he told the *gastralyor*

blew in these Novgorod scum to the local *pandilleros* before they could administer the promised *bit repu* upon him, and not interested in a gunfight at the end of the world the two punks flew away diseased crows

by (admittedly mixed) virtue of this episode growing in stature among *los pandilleros*, primed already by their holy mothers to think him *un santo* despite witnessing him evenings drinking *cervesa* and cackling in *el lupanar* with a whore on his lap

his totem the flightless cormorant (*Nannopterum harrisi*), dream diver, of all the world's cormorants the only one that has lost the ability to fly, and the only one found in the Galapagos

escritor de sueño moves as if floating before the Seminario, ancient creatures whispering to him and he to them; still sometimes levitating alone in the studio as night falls over the gulf of Guayaquil

made her way slowly (*quick quick* he says in English) down the stony path behind the house in Pílos to the sun-bleached shack looking out on the sea at a distance below

3 September, Pílos (Pylos) Greece N35deg 48.25sec, E21deg 38.86sec

standing before her table at the taverna by the bay in Finikounda introduced himself the way old men in foreign countries sometimes do

Tamas

Thomas?

Tamas, is different, mean twin English, *gemelos, gemelli, capische?*

eating a broiled fish whose name she could not understand fresh from the Kaikia drawn up along the sandy shore at midday, a flinty cold bottle of Hymettos, casting an eye up at him through wraparound lilac lenses

binièta Tamas he kept saying, at first she thought it his name

thought he might be holding bouquets of anemones like an arab vendor

ghia' Tamas ghia' nice to meet you

binièta Tamas binièta

pantomimes writing index finger like a pen over his palm

binièta Tamas vignetta (frustrated)

after she gave him a Staedtler 01 pen from her rucksack smiling took her hand, surprisingly soft palm for what she thought a sailor, a flush of excitement at being taken up so even by a white haired man with eyes bluer than the sea

quick sketch of a credible boat hull and shore line, a sense of trees, dark ink like a tattoo against the tan the pen tickling slightly

beta iota nu iota epsilon tau alpha: carefully scratched calligraphy

below it enscribing a second caption: v-i-g-n-e-t-t-a

perhaps under the impression she was Italian since she could not stop saying *certo* or *si* after a month of sailing there before this

binièta he patted the back of her hand, a gesture to match his whisper, before freeing her

binièta I show

a guide she thought and declined, pointing toward the boat

sailing, she said

si, si, everyone sailing, ten meters Kaikia, he said, *binièta* I show, *enta'ksi?* OK?

Ok, she said because she was alone and he had held her hand

sitting without her bidding he joined her at the table waiting while she quickly finished the fish, refusing both a portion or a glass of wine; but when she pushed the plate away wanting to get on with it, used her spoon and fork to expertly extricate two morsels of flesh from the head of the fish, sliding the plate back toward her paternally, indicating she should eat

tesori he said treasures *gioiello guancia*

fish cheeks

waited by his pitted and faded pea green 60's vintage Italian motor scooter while she checked the boat, picking up the sat phone from the sea locker just in case and leaving a note in the ship's log:

3 September 14:56: (Finikounda) leaving with a man named Tamas to see binièta, why I do not know

stomach muscles a hard band where she held on at his waist bouncing along roads not on any map, tufted patches penning goats and roosters under blue skies, brilliant white houses, air fragrant with wildflowers, oregano, and lemon trees, a woman in black hanging bleached white sheets on a line, lapis lazuli vistas of unrippled sea

somewhere along a rim of hills above Pilos his whitewashed two story house like the others, garden somewhat overgrown, windows shuttered, alarmed at its remoteness she makes a phone call leaving a message on a friend's phone in Prague remaining by the scooter as he goes inside

"not coming" she shouts after, "*efcharisto'* thank you," but he does not hear, emerging after some time with a terracotta pitcher of water and two clay cups, the water sweet and cool even without ice, motioning her down the scrub hill (quick, quick) to the shack which he opened, beckoning her enter

still not trusting (herself or him?) lingering in the doorway nonetheless gasped when he opened a high shutter bathing the secret room in midday light

jeweled spectrum within fragrant dark wood, the carefully
fitted boards of polished rosewood covered over ceiling to
floor with layers of richly coloured and undulant surface of
roadway vignettes, luggage stickers and city emblems, *binièta*
from all over (Italia, Deutschland, Suiza, Monaco, California
U. S., he recited a brief census), the swirling overlay of engraved patches decoupaged with a gold substance like honey,
resin or wax, a glowing collage of baroque decoration, finally more Italian than Greek

ché stanza bella! she sighed, unable to keep from the wrong
language

A ogni uccello il suo nido è bello, he replied proudly, an Italian
proverb: every bird thinks its own nest is beautiful

kallisto she whispered praying that was the right word

drive camion, truck, 18 wheels (smiles proudly), all over for
fifty year, even to Manchester, London, Baghdad, Istanbul

shook her head vigorously understanding, yes, yes, *parakalo'
kalime'ra*, she wanted to say thank you great but suspected she
had maybe said goodnight

my wife he die four year now, before bring *binièta* from every
country for her smiling

efcharisto' efcharisto', he said, kissing the back of her hand
where he had drawn the vignette upon it

she found herself wordlessly crying

maybe you marry? he asked and she could not tell if it was meant as a proposal or a prophecy

back down to the shore along precarious roads she held him tight around the waist, sometimes burying her face against the sweet smelling cotton, whispering yes, yes, in memory

bright December morning a week before solstice and the vineyard pruners in olive-colored coveralls and matching berets move the smoking *brouette* between the rows on which they work, orange battery packs on their back black lines of the *secateurs*, electrical pruning knives, fastened to a cuff at the bicep, umbilicals trailing down to the trigger grips, cane-clippers

man and wife although one could not tell from a distance

sun burns off the low mist after a night of frost and is re-placed by the smoke from the Sauvignon canes burning in the *brouette*

trail of grey ash where the burning cart has been

from the first of December to the spring solstice *on taille les vignes*, carving a coming time out of winter, twelve hectares of old vines here and another seventeen closer to the *loges de vigne*

are they in love? one cannot say although even here they are tender to each other by habit weeks are long and months drag on and it is difficult to bring imagination to weary lovemaking

J'avais l'habitude de savoir mille manières de faire l'amour mais maintenant je suis prévisible, sondage

once knowing a thousand ways of making love he's turned predictable, boring, he complains

her laugh carrying in the cold morning air

Comment pense-tu à ces choses? how do you think of this stuff, she says, patting his unshaven cheek with her free hand

pats her ass in return, *un prêté pour un rendu,* tit for tat

starts predictably enough she supposes but soon becomes an intricate inebriated ceremony, a courtly swooning she imagines as the way fancy men and women walk near each other along a garden path or how *les hirondelles* wheel wing to wing above the Loire

Où la chèvre est attachée, il faut qu'elle broute.

a goat grazes where she is tethered

smiles at him, to think of making love before midmorning, sap still rising in the old vines

returns to the rows

was

mille manières de faire, mille badines des vignes

we do what we do she thinks

deep in the eyes of the jaundiced baby splayed like an old
hen in the plastic incubator are dreams the old doctor tells
himself

creature tied to a nest of wires and tubes, digital dials and
fantastic lights and streams of cool air, and yet its deepest
being and fantastic visions show upon no screen nor can be
uttered

able to save them now when they are no bigger than kittens,
as furless, as helplessly mewing

and raise them up to what? he thinks what heights? what
words encompass when all this travail is forgotten replaced
by a succession of pains, unimaginable heartbreaks, the
boredom

once renting a villa in Umbria cracked an egg and an em-
bryo fell into the bowl, the housekeeper at his elbow already
affronted *il dottore* presumed to cook himself a frittata crossing herself frantically to ward off the *mal'occhio*

scrawny creature afloat in the glistening eggwhites

life itself a surprise

they say we die alone but that can't be she thinks, has given
birth nine times and lost two to time and circumstance but

thinks all things must be reconciled eventually, thinks thinks she thinks, relieved, wave on wave reaching far shores, even granite cliffs melting like lozenges (Edward Weston photograph Point Lobos 1947), the batter and caress of pain cresting with the morphine, jadelike glinting low along ophite porphyry, spume and plume (perfume!), the rhymed delight in tidal music, fingers circling over buttock, flank, and inner hollow, moan and curlew call was once

nous perdants, loose and losing, descends from cave to cave, pushing ever lower damply, a dew my darlings, baby at the breast before the milk is in

where   have   we   come   from   where   are   we   going

•